Louise

SARAH LAMB

ISBN: 979-8-9867275-8-5

Contents

To my own little sister…

Chapter 1

Southampton, United Kingdom, April 1912

Louise forced her tapping fingers to still. The anxiousness she felt kept bursting out, and so she looked for a distraction. Luckily, her younger sister, Mathilda, could be one. Louise couldn't help but smile at how enthusiastically her sister was reading the newspaper.

After Mathilda had discovered the mail-order bride advertisements yesterday, she'd hardly stopped giggling. Since the hotel had so many newspapers—ones from all over the world—there had been almost a never-ending supply for her to pore over.

Nearly rolling her eyes at the one her sister was currently reading, Louise let her gaze roam the hotel room, lingering on the window where people scurried past in a never-ending stream. How busy it was here.

Inside, the sisters enjoyed a luxurious suite of rooms, whose comfort far surpassed any place the two of them had been for a long time.

It was obvious the hotel was used to travelers from all over, as the newspaper her sister was browsing was from the United States, and the state of Kentucky. Louise marveled at the fact the hotel had hundreds of newspapers for their guests, from every state, several countries and, of course, from all over England. When she'd rung for newspapers to be brought up to give them something to do, she hadn't expected so many to be delivered.

Some of the mail-order bride advertisements were quite sad. Louise felt sympathetic toward those as her sister read them out loud. It was a terrifying thing to put your future in the hands of someone you didn't know. The women placing these ads were brave. How did one find the courage to become a mail-order bride? In truth, she felt little more than one herself, though she'd never admit it to Mathilda.

Her eyes landed on one of the ad headlines. *Seeking a man of wealth.*

Aren't we all, Louise thought dryly.

Dropping a few sugar cubes in her tea, an indulgence which had long been denied as sugar was expensive, she leaned close, pretending to read along with her sister. In reality, she was trying to calm her nerves.

At any moment, the man she was to marry would walk in. She'd never met Mr. Hillcock. They'd exchanged a few letters, but that was it. She wondered if he'd be the same as his letters. Bland. Short. Uninteresting.

When each envelope arrived with a new one, it didn't fill her with the feelings she had always imagined as a young girl. Instead of being eager and excited and in love, she was filled with dread. The only good thing was she had been promised Mr. Hillcock was a man of means, and would provide generously for her, and perhaps her sister. That's the only reason she had agreed.

Mathilda said something, and Louise forced herself to pay attention. "Mm?"

"Not every woman can be as successful in marriage as you will be," Mathilda said, slumping in her chair with a dejected expression. "Do you think I'll ever be, Lou?"

Louise studied her for a moment. *Dear one, it's all I pray for, and why I'm doing this. You deserve happiness.*

However, instead of voicing her thoughts, Louise raised an eyebrow, something she was quite good at, and replied, "Not if you don't improve your posture and your attitude. Really, Mattie. You'd think you never had a governess."

Her sister sighed deeply and straightened in the chair, then peered at the paper, her face brightening. "This one is terribly amusing, Louise. I suspect it will make you laugh."

"I doubt that," Louise said, though she hoped it would. "Try me." She leaned forward slightly, trying to spot which advertisement her sister was referring to.

"Wanted," Mathilda read in a solemn, theatrical voice, "a wife who can skin a hog and pluck a chicken faster than I can."

Louise's lips twitched and she lowered her tea before giggles took over and she spilled it. The image the advertisement created was quite hilarious. Would the man really be auditioning women to see who could pluck a chicken faster than him?

"I almost made you smile!" her sister said happily, her eyes bright.

Together, they read a few more. One was incredibly sad and made Louise feel melancholy. It had read, "I am young and have no fortune other than that of my good looks and disposition. In me you will find a loyal wife, should you treat me kindly."

Though she didn't know the young woman who'd written the ad, Louise felt she understood her well. Life could be terribly unfair sometimes.

There was a knock, and Louise's body tensed. A lump formed in her throat and traveled its way down to her stomach, where it sat as heavily as the plum pudding she'd tried to make last Christmas. It had turned out quite badly. Just like this marriage might.

She drew in a sharp breath. Thinking like that would only get things off to a poor start. *Be positive, Louise.*

The parlor door opened, and a maid from the hotel walked in. "Miss," she said, dropping a curtsy to Louise. "Mr. Hillcock is here."

"Thank you," Louise said, and waved the maid away. She stood and looked at her reflection in the large mirror over the hotel suite's mantle. Adjusting the ribbon at her throat, her only adornment as the last of her jewelry was sold the year before, she turned this way and that, then nodded to her sister.

A strange heaviness had settled over the room, and it was obvious Mathilda felt it as well. Her sister bore a serious expression as she watched her anxiously. Louise raised both brows this time, giving her sister a pointed look.

"I'll show him in," Mathilda said, rising from her seat.

As her sister left, Louise perched on one of the overstuffed chairs set around a small table. Swallowing hard, she tried to ignore the flutter of fear swirling around in her stomach.

I'm doing this for us. I'm doing this for Mattie.

That's what she'd done for the last several years—all she could, so that her younger sister would have a better life. Things had been difficult and she was tired of the struggles and sacrifices they'd had to make. So why, when this opportunity had presented itself, did she not feel more at ease with it?

After Mama died, Father had drunk himself to death. Somehow, he'd also gone terribly into debt, his lawyer told them at Father's funeral. There was the house, but not much else.

A very small allowance had been given to Louise and Mathilda, but for two girls who had been raised with the best, it wasn't enough. Louise had been forced to leave finishing school when Mama had died, and Mathilda's governess had been dismissed, as had their staff. The sisters had to learn to care for themselves, but it was one thing learning to manage with one parent still around to seek advice from, and another when suddenly all on your own.

It was nearly impossible to provide anything more than the essentials on that meager allowance. Louise reflected on how it had been a long time since either of them had a new dress or shoes, or even something frivolous. When the lawyer suggested she marry a wealthy man, and offered to introduce her to one of his clients, Louise had felt an immense rush of gratitude.

Of course, immediately afterward it was followed by an intense fear, but each time she looked at her younger sister, Louise pushed that aside. If she pretended all was well, perhaps it would turn out to be that way. Mattie was younger than her and deserved happiness. That was something that she could provide with a good marriage. Having wealth would allow her to find a husband for Mattie, and potentially even a love match.

Love was something that Louise could never afford to have, and she knew it. Survival came before love. There had never been warmth in any of the letters sent to her, though she'd tried to give affection she didn't feel. She knew it was unlikely there would be any romance in this marriage.

As a twenty-five-year-old spinster, she should be grateful for this chance, their father's lawyer had said. Louise was, though it didn't mean her pride wasn't bruised. If things had been different, she'd have surely been married before now, with a family and a home of her own, and perhaps even children.

Louise looked up and saw her sister standing in front of the closed parlor door, lost in daydreams. She gave a small cough, and Mathilda startled, gave a sheepish grin with a shrug, and disappeared through the door.

Biting her lip, Louise allowed herself to wonder, not for the first time that hour, what Mr. Hillcock would be like. He couldn't be all bad. They were honeymooning on the *Titanic* after a small wedding in the hotel before embarking. Any man who could manage to get tickets for this ship, as well as plan a prestigious honeymoon aboard it, must care about comforts and appearances.

Wistfully, Louise thought of her wedding dress. It wasn't at all what she'd dreamed about as a girl, something frilly with a long train. No, this was simple. As the wedding would be. But she'd make sure that her sister had everything she desired for hers.

The whole thing had happened so rapidly, there had been no time to plan. She supposed that was fortunate, but it wasn't long at all after the lawyer had made the introduction by mail that Louise and Mathilda had found themselves in Southampton, England. Mathilda had gone as a chaperone, but would return home once Louise was married.

Louise hoped it wouldn't be long before she found someone suitable for her sister. She worried about her being alone in the crumbling house, filled with memories and trophies from their father's explorations.

Faint voices drew closer. Nervously, Louise waited, but not for long. A tall man with a scar on one side of his face stalked in the room, gave her a brisk nod of his head, and said, "Louise. We meet at last."

A practiced smile forming, Louise rose and held her hand out. As damp lips kissed it in welcome, she saw Mathilda sit in a chair across the room, holding her book and pretending to read. Louise knew it was pretend; the book was upside down. She wondered if Mathilda would notice.

"How was your journey?" Mr. Hillcock asked, taking a seat near her.

Louise settled back in her own. "It was tiresome, but this hotel is restoring my comfort and I feel much more rested. Thank you for providing the suite for Mathilda and me."

"It was my pleasure," Mr. Hillcock answered. "The two of you will join me for dinner in the hotel restaurant tonight. My business associate will also join us."

"That sounds lovely," Louise said.

He reached into a pocket. "I'm also entrusting our tickets to board the *Titanic* to you."

"My goodness," Louise said, surprised he was handing her something so important. "I will take care of them."

Perhaps she'd been worried for nothing. Mr. Hillcock was a little stiff in his way, but they hardly knew each other. It was to be expected. A tiny flicker of hope formed.

Then she looked at the tickets and frowned. "These aren't the correct names. Is there a mistake?"

The look he gave her was one of pity. "No one travels using their real names," he said, condescension in his tone. "It isn't fashionable."

"Oh, of course not," Louise said, laughing lightly. "You must forgive me. It's been quite some time since I've been in proper company. My sister and I have kept to ourselves for far too long."

Mr. Hillcock rose and the scent of his overly strong hair tonic assaulted her nose. "It's understandable. Your life will be much different now." He gave her a severe look. "You are expected to know how my class lives, but until you do, keep quiet and don't say foolish things."

Louise's breath caught. She ducked her head and nodded. "Of course," she murmured. "Forgive me."

Mr. Hillcock's dark eyes seemed to bore into her. "You'll learn soon enough," he said, his voice so low it would not carry beyond the two of them. "I expect perfection. I will rid you of your lower-class habits, even if I must beat them out of you."

He looked at her once more, and her skin crawled as she met his soulless eyes. "Don't be late for dinner. I'm sure you can manage that?"

He turned, and Louise closed her eyes for the briefest of moments. The hope that had sparked was now snuffed out. Mr. Hillcock was not what she'd expected. He was much, much worse.

Chapter 2

"I don't really care for him," Mathilda confessed as Mr. Hillcock left and the two sisters were alone again.

Louise agreed entirely, but how could she say so? Her sister continued, always one to speak her mind.

"He is handsome enough, I suppose, except for the scar on his face. But he never seemed at ease, almost like he was hiding something or ready to leave a party he doesn't like. And he uses entirely too much hair tonic."

With a nod, Louise pressed her lips together. It was a rather strong smell. She hoped he wouldn't wear it often around her. Perhaps she could gift him a new bottle in a more pleasing scent. The hotel might sell one.

She didn't feel like talking, but if she didn't say something to end the conversation, Mathilda might go on forever. She couldn't bear to hear any more critical things. Already, she loathed the idea of being with the man. That he expected perfection from her, and would demand it by striking her, filled Louise with terror.

Taking a deep breath, Louise answered briskly, "Nor do I, but that's beside the point. Women in our circumstances cannot be choosy. But at least we have choices, and better options than those women in the newspaper." She gestured toward the table, the newspapers spread over the top.

Mathilda nodded as Louise continued to talk, but Louise could see her sister's dejected face and knew that Mattie must be worried for her own future. Of course she was. It was bad enough that Louise was going to have to wed a man like Mr. Hillcock. What must Mathilda think was in store for her?

Her voice softened, "It will work out, Mattie. He is well off in business and travels a great deal. It is expected I will either go along and see the world, or explore my own interests at home. Neither is bad. It is really quite a fortunate match."

Mathilda didn't look up from her lap. Louise felt unwanted tears burn in her eyes. She wouldn't cry. It was her job to do whatever it took to take care of her sister. This was just one more thing. She bit her cheek hard, the pain removing the emotion that threatened to sound in her voice.

Reaching an arm around Mathilda, Louise gave her a little squeeze. With a smile, she said in a practiced light voice, "This will also allow me the opportunity to find a husband for you. I'll be in a better position to help you find all you seek. I will try, dear Mattie, for someone who is all that you could have ever wanted."

Mathilda didn't answer, but returned the embrace and nodded. Her expression looked more at ease, and her eyes roamed toward the cookies on the nearby table.

Her mouth dry, Louise checked the teapot and poured. Feeling extravagant, she stirred in several lumps of sugar. That, at least, had better be one thing she could have plenty of in her marriage. Hot, bracing tea, and unlimited sugar. As mistress of their house, she'd insist upon it.

And hope Mr. Hillcock agreed.

She realized her sister was talking again. "I find it strange he doesn't want you to use his first name, only Mr. Hillcock," Mathilda said. "Do you even know it? Doesn't that seem odd?"

Louise hesitated before answering. What could she say that would both set her sister's mind at ease, and her own? She mumbled a reply and drunk deeply from her tea.

"Mmm," Mathilda answered, but her look was skeptical. Her face brightened then. "May I see the tickets?"

Louise nodded and walked over to her handbag. She was surprised it had taken Mathilda so long to ask. Her younger sister was nearly obsessed with the Ship of Dreams, as the newspapers referred to it.

It seemed the *Titanic* was always in the newspaper. There was talk of the chair filled decks, a long promenade, Turkish baths, food made by the finest of chefs, and the incredible wonders of the majestic ship not even shared yet with the public.

Mathilda ran a finger along a ticket's edge. "You are terribly lucky, Lou!" Then she frowned and looked up. "Is there a mistake? These tickets. They are for a Louis and Martha Smith."

"Don't make faces," Louise scolded. "You'll wrinkle sooner." Taking the tickets, she looked at them once more and tucked them back into her handbag. Clasping it, she returned it to the mantle above the fireplace.

Mr. Hillcock's earlier words crept into her mind, and the shame she felt at his tone made her stomach feel sick. Still, she turned back to her sister with a smile and a casual wave of her hand. "You silly thing. It's fashionable to travel under a different name. You'd be surprised how many wealthy people do it."

Ending the conversation, Louise yawned. "I'm going to rest for a while. We are going to have dinner tonight with Mr. Hillcock and his business associate."

Louise suggested a dress for Mathilda, wanting to avoid any unpleasantness with Mr. Hillcock. Her body felt tight, tense with anxiety, and she hoped her sister wouldn't see as she walked away. Let Mathilda think what she would, that she was tired, or excited to pack. The truth was far different.

With her door safely locked, Louise buried her face in the softest pillow she'd ever rested her head on and cried. Tears, hot and bitter, flowed, wetting the pillow and reddening her eyes. She cried for the unfairness of the situation, for her fears, and for her sister.

At last, without a drop of moisture left in her eyes, Louise stood, threw her shoulders back, and faced herself in the mirror. Her pale face with just a hint of freckles and hazel eyes stared back. Dampening a towel from her washbasin, Louise dabbed her face until the redness faded.

"Your tears are done," she told herself in a low voice. "From now on, no tears and no regrets. You will do what you must do. For Mathilda, and for yourself. Do what you must to survive, no matter the cost."

Chapter 3

Dressed in a dark blue gown with almost no embellishment, Louise turned before the mirror. She'd brushed her hair until it gleamed, then fixed it herself. Piled high upon her head, it was elegant. Though she didn't have any jewelry right now, it wasn't needed, not with nature's gifts—soft eyes, full lips, and a serene expression. The headmistress at her boarding school had taught the girls that.

"You might face times when you have only your natural charms to rely upon," Mrs. Harris had said. *"Remember, they are no less a gift than an expensive necklace. The eyes, lips, and face can show many expressions. Always keep yours relaxed and with a hint of a smile."*

Louise leaned slightly closer to the mirror and reflected upon herself. She looked calm, poised, and radiant.

The exact opposite of how she felt. Mrs. Harris would be proud that her lessons had stuck.

Though the meal was sure to be delicious, she wondered if she could manage to eat any of it. Raising her chin slightly, she glided into the outer room.

Mathilda was dressed as well, and staring through the window. Her younger sister was restless. She could tell. Both of them enjoyed their long walks, but here, they'd been told to stay indoors. Louise wondered if that was so they wouldn't get lost or because Mr. Hillcock demanded it simply to keep an eye on her.

Clearing her throat, as not to startle her sister, she asked, "Are you ready?"

Mathilda turned and nodded. "Ready. Will Mr. Hillcock be escorting us down?"

"No," Louise said. *Thankfully. His presence at dinner will be enough for the day.* "We are to meet him there. He's made a reservation. Come, we don't want to be late." She plucked up her handbag and strode toward the door.

Mathilda was scrambling behind her. "I thought it was fashionable to be late?"

Mr. Hillcock's warning echoed in Louise's mind. Mattie was right, since often the two had to walk everywhere, at times they were a few moments late. It was acceptable, back home. With Mr. Hillcock, it seemed it wasn't.

She put on her best lecturing tone as she led them to the stairway and down a corridor. "Fashionable, yes. Rude? Also yes."

Mathilda didn't answer. Louise might not have even heard her if she did. The hotel lobby opened before them in a magnificence she'd missed. Being without means could be quite dull, especially after a life of having had only the best. Here, she felt in her domain, back in her comfort zone.

Everything was white marble. Plush chairs and small sofas also in white lined the walls, and a small fountain surrounded by ferns and small white flowers formed a centerpiece for the lobby. From the ceiling to the floor, everything gleamed brightly as hints of gold entwined with the white. It was almost an ethereal sort of scene, Louise felt, as she led them toward the restaurant.

They passed a painting of a fox hunt and Louise stumbled. Turning her head, she hurried past it. The image it provoked was one she didn't want. It reminded her too much of her mother, and of the accident that had taken her away.

Many years ago, she and Mathilda stayed in places like this with their family. Those were also the days she had more dresses than could be counted, and two parents who loved them and gave them a comfortable lifestyle. If only that had not all changed in an instant. What might she and Mathilda be doing today?

With the restaurant only a few steps away, Louise took Mathilda's arm. Her little sister was all she had left, and she'd do what she could to protect her. Mathilda had their mother's honest way of speaking. There wasn't a deceptive bone in her body. She also had their mother's eyes.

They passed another painting of a fox hunt. Were the wretched things everywhere? She could never pass one without thinking of her mother. Their beautiful mother had died after a riding accident during a fox hunt. The horse shied from a jump, or perhaps got spooked, and threw her. Afterward, their father had hidden himself away until his death. Louise knew it was from grief, but had felt all but abandoned.

A man in a suit greeted them, blessedly distracting her. "Ladies?"

"Mr. Hillcock's party," Louise quietly murmured.

"Follow me," he said with a small bow, and led them into a large dining room. At a table near the rear, Mr. Hillcock sat, along with another man. Both rose at their approach.

"Louise, my darling," Mr. Hillcock said, reaching for her hand. "Don't you look lovely."

"Thank you," Louise said, lowering her eyelashes and ducking her head. The gesture seemed to please him, for he patted her hand and pulled out her chair.

"I'm Mr. Longsmith," the other man said, leaning over Mathilda to smile. "You two are just as Mr. Hillcock said."

"Let's order," Mr. Hillcock said, saving Louise from thinking of a reply. He handed her a menu. "Order what you like. We are celebrating, you know."

"That is very generous of you," Louise said, relaxing slightly at the nod of approval he gave her.

When the waiter returned, she ordered a meal of chicken, roasted potatoes, and green peas.

Mr. Longsmith took up the conversation. Louise tried not to stare or frown. Something about him felt familiar, but she couldn't think what. It nudged her mind in an uncomfortable way.

"So, tell me, ladies. How are you enjoying the area?"

Louise didn't have to give more than a polite answer, as Mathilda started talking about the *Titanic*. The girl could talk for days about it, and it seemed Mr. Longsmith could as well. That was fortunate, for it allowed Louise to simply smile, nod, and give the occasional comment.

Their food arrived, and it was as every bit scrumptious as she could have hoped. Though the knot in her stomach that had formed after meeting

Mr. Hillcock hadn't left, thankfully it allowed her sustenance.

Mr. Hillcock insisted upon dessert, which she and Mathilda accepted. Louise was served strawberries in fresh cream. She enjoyed each and thanked Mr. Hillcock again.

It was obvious he enjoyed the flattery and her attention. She must remember that. Perhaps things would go better for her if she played the mild, sweet, subservient woman who, in truth, she was nothing like.

There was a guffaw of laughter, and Mr. Longsmith tossed down his napkin. "Reminds me of our days in Mexico, doesn't it, Frankie my boy?"

Louise startled, but didn't look up. Frankie? Frank? The lawyer had said Mr. Hillcock's name was Albert. Which was it?

Raising her glass of water, she took a quick look over the rim and saw Mr. Hillcock's raised brow pointed at his partner. The other man recovered, sputtering, "Yes, Frankie was quite a chap, good tour guide, wasn't he, Mr. Hillcock?"

"Indeed," the dry reply came.

Louise returned her glass to the table and took the opportunity to glance again at Mr. Longsmith.

The other man was stocky and also overused hair tonic. Unlike Mr. Hillcock, his eyes were friendly and jovial, but she had the feeling it was an act. Whereas her future husband was nothing but steel, and didn't mind showing it, Mr. Longsmith seemed to hide his true personality behind humor.

"Shall we call it an evening?" Mr. Hillcock said suddenly, dropping his napkin onto the table. "I have a few things I must take care of before we set sail."

"Of course," Louise said. She gave him an easy smile, one that all girls were taught their first week of boarding school. "It's been a delightful meal."

He rose and she followed. Mathilda and Mr. Longsmith also stood. "We shall escort you to the stairway," Mr. Hillcock said, leaving no room for argument.

Louise inclined her head and picked up her handbag. They walked into the lobby. It was more crowded than when she and Mathilda had come down. Little clusters of guests stood around. As they passed by one, she heard an older man gasp. "By jove, isn't that man the spitting image of that chap the police are looking for?"

If she tensed, she hoped she covered it by stumbling into her sister. "Forgive me," she said. "My shoe slipped."

Mattie smiled, unaware of the ruse, and took her arm. "I shall hold you then," she laughed merrily. "New shoes always do the same for me!"

Behind them, Mr. Hillcock and Mr. Longsmith still walked, their voices low. The men were not quite with them, but also not leaving them to walk alone. Louise had the sinking suspicion it was on purpose. Had they heard the man's gasp?

She paused at the stairs, and a breath later, Mr. Hillcock arrived. "Goodnight," he said, with a small bow.

Mr. Longsmith approached Mathilda much the same, and as he bowed, his shirt collar bunched. Louise caught sight of a small tattoo on his neck. With a rush of fear, she knew now where she'd seen him.

Somehow, she and Mathilda said goodnight and made it to their room before she collapsed. Once the door was closed, Louise paced furiously, her mind comparing the facts and the suspicions.

Mathilda timidly approached her, and Louise stared at her younger sister. Questions whirled in her mind, each hurling themselves as an accusation. *How could she have let this happen to them? How could she have let this happen to Mattie? What kind of sister was she, leading them into the hands of men like this?*

"Lou," Mathilda asked, her tone one of concern, "what's wrong?"

Louise moved faster, almost frantically. Could she tell her? Should she tell her? She must say something, but what would they do? Finally, she faced her sister. "Mattie, I've made a terrible mistake," she whispered. A whisper seemed all she was capable of. Her mouth was so dry. Was there any tea left?

"The marriage? But I thought—"

"Shh. Keep your voice low," Louise interrupted. She pulled her sister close, and almost hissed, "Do you know who that Mr. Longsmith is? Do you recognize him?" Her tone came out harsher than she'd intended.

Mathilda shook her head. "No. Who is he?"

Her voice trembling, and her fingers gripping her sister's forearms tightly, Louise whispered, "That's no one other than the notorious gangster, Long John."

She could tell Mathilda was trying to recall the name. Her sister read as much as she did, perhaps more, and both had devoured each newspaper they could get their hands on. No longer a part of society, it was their only link to staying sane, and to keeping abreast of the latest news.

With realization, Mathilda gasped, and it was her turn to grab Louise's arms. She brought her head close. "The one who is tied up in counterfeiting and the Federal Bureau of Investigation is after? Do you think Mr. Hillcock is his partner?"

Before Louise could answer, there was a knock at the door. She'd not even had time to register the sound when a hotel maid entered. Behind the woman, Mr. Hillcock strode in, carrying a briefcase and wearing an expression Louise couldn't decipher. Had he overheard her?

Chapter 4

Louise wiped the fear off of her face, replacing it with a welcoming smile. *Thank you, finishing school.* "What a surprise," she said, her tone sweet. Though her heart was hammering so loudly she worried it might burst from her chest, she walked to her betrothed. *Had he overheard her?*

She continued to prattle, keeping her tone light to allay any suspicion and perhaps even calm her own nerves. "I'm grateful I wasn't in my dressing gown yet! Have you come to relax with some tea? I can order to the room." Louise turned to call for the hotel staff.

"No, I've not the time," Mr. Hillcock said, and she paused and turned back to him.

Nearby, Mathilda was watching, almost staring, and Louise arched a brow at her sister. Mathilda flushed and looked at her shoes.

Mr. Hillcock said something, and it took her a moment to register he was talking, "… must assist with a last-minute business deal before the *Titanic* sails. Just meet me on the dock."

"Oh, of course," Louise said, nodding. "I will make sure to have my trunks sent ahead. Will we still be married before we embark?"

If she could escape before they were married, perhaps she could find a way to hide herself and Mattie. Louise held her breath as she waited for his answer.

"There won't be time. We shall do it upon the ship. I'll arrange for it. Do you have some paper?" Mr. Hillcock asked, his eyes darting around once more. "I need to leave a note for someone."

"Oh, yes, of course. Mattie, darling, can you please help Mr. Hillcock?" Louise asked as Mr. Hillcock set down his briefcase on the table next to her. The clasp loosened as he set it down, and inside she could see a large stack of papers and a thick pile of cash. Anger suddenly surged. Father's lawyer had promised money for her and Mathilda's journey, but had given it to Mr. Hillcock for safe keeping. She and Mathilda had nearly had to beg to be allowed a few dollars for food on their journey, and here he had all of this?

She was determined to get some of it back. Louise kept one eye on Mathilda as her sister led him over to the desk in the far side of the room. The moment his back was turned, she plunged her hand inside of his briefcase, and pulled it out again, a stack of money in her hand.

Mathilda saw, and Louise gave a tiny shake of her head. Mathilda stood before Mr. Hillcock and reached out slightly, drawing his attention. Louise was about to return some of the money when another stack of papers, each different in color and size and handwritings caught her eye. Near the top was her father's lawyer's name, and for some reason she couldn't possibly explain, she pushed her hand into the briefcase once more, pulled out another pile of the papers, then clasped the briefcase closed.

If she'd thought her heart was racing before, it was about to burst out of her chest now. Louise was sure she was flushed. She could hardly breathe, her chest was so tight.

Mr. Hillcock was turning. *What to do?* Louise yanked the silk flowers out of the vase in front of her, and pretended to rearrange them, turning her head to the side slightly, while pushing the papers and the cash deep inside the empty vase.

Mr. Hillcock approached. The briefcase was closed, and he didn't even look at it as he picked it up and strode toward the door.

Louise said a soft goodbye and closed it behind him. She stood at the door and waited a long moment, then opened it again, peering out until she was sure she and Mathilda were alone before turning back to her sister. Her legs felt shaky, but she didn't acknowledge them.

"Pack quickly," she ordered. "Also, take a small bag with your essentials, just in case."

"Lou…" Mathilda bit down on her lip.

Louise didn't answer. Instead, she reached into the flower vase. Still keeping her voice low, she said,

"I took these. Some of it is mine. Our lawyer gave it to him for safekeeping and my expenses, so I don't feel bad. Tomorrow, we leave, you and I."

Her sister wore an expression of fear mixed with disbelief. Louise wasn't sure if it was from her words or from the absolute fortune in front of them.

Louise continued, "We mustn't make it look suspicious. You'll go in the morning to sightsee. Take only what you can carry, but then board the *Titanic*. I'll send your luggage on with mine."

Now it was her sister's turn to pace. Mathilda took several steps, then turned back, twisting her fingers with an anxious expression on her face. "If Mr. Hillcock and his associate are gangsters, they will know something is missing from the briefcase and will come after it. Possibly tonight."

Mathilda was right. She hadn't thought of that. Briefly closing her eyes, she willed her mind to work faster. After a moment, she shook her head. "I doubt it. I didn't take all the money, nor all the papers. At a glance, there's no way to tell it's not there. Also, it's late. I doubt he will look into his case. Tomorrow we will hide. They won't be able to find us as they can't board the ship without tickets," Louise said. With a reassuring look, she reached out and squeezed Mathilda's arm, then crossed the room over to the desk.

Sitting at the chair, she took up the hotel pen and some pieces of paper. She scribbled on one, and then on a second, glancing over at the newspaper on the desk Mathilda had discarded earlier.

There was no other choice. They were in a country they didn't know, far from anyone who might be able to help them, and now, with criminals chasing them. They had to disguise themselves. Louise only hoped it worked.

Her shoulders tense, Louise looked once more at the newspaper advertisements and, with resolution, folded the notes. She stood and held them out to her sister.

Mathilda accepted them with an uncertain look on her face.

Reaching for her sister's handbag, Louise motioned for her to put the notes inside and Louise continued with her plan. "You'll go in the morning and take these to a telegraph station. Don't do it here at the hotel. There's a place to send these right outside of the dock, I suspect."

Mathilda looked down at the papers and gasped once she read them. "Are you serious?"

With a bitter look, Louisa nodded. There was nothing else to do. "Yes. You, Mathilda, are about to be the bride of a small-town man. And myself? I'm going to work sums for a shopkeeper and care for a young child."

Chapter 5

Louise pressed her lips together. Mathilda was sitting in a chair in a complete panic. This really wasn't the time. They were in a dire situation, and it was possible that her younger sister didn't realize how serious it was.

"You can't escape people like that. We'll end up in the newspaper! As murdered!" Mathilda said, her voice rising to almost a squeak.

Ah, she did realize the seriousness. Louise had the same fear, but this was her fault, her mess, and she had to find the solution and keep her sister alive. Even if it was less than ideal.

* * *

Louise watched closely as her bags and Mathilda's were labeled by the hotel staff. She'd put them all under her name. Not that they had many. After being assured, again, they'd arrive safely on the *Titanic*, she took Mathilda's arm and strolled along the corridor, down the stairs, and through the lobby.

Her pace was even, though she forced herself to look calm and relaxed. She had to. Mathilda seemed as though she was trembling, which is why she linked arms with her.

Stopping at the hotel front desk, Louise asked, in a voice a little louder than usual, "I need to get a new hat. Can you point me to the best shop, please?"

She didn't really pay attention to the answer, but she thanked the man and left, then stopped and asked a passing woman, "My dear! Your handbag is divine! I must have one in blue. Pray, where did you purchase it?"

As the woman answered, she felt Mathilda tighten her grip. Ignoring her sister, she thanked the woman and breezily resumed her walk, stopping once more to ask the doorman to direct her to the closest department store. "I simply must have a new dress," she declared.

By this time, Mathilda was flat out staring at her, and Louise jabbed her in the ribs. They walked around the corner of the hotel, and Louise near dragged her to a park she'd seen from the window.

Reaching into her handbag, she pulled out the *Titanic* ticket for Martha Smith and a stack of money. "Here." She shoved it into Mathilda's hand. "Do you have the messages to wire?"

"I do," Mathilda said.

"Good. Send them and get on the ship. I'll find you soon." Louise turned to leave, but looked back at her sister's question.

"Are you sure this will work?" Mathilda asked. "I thought we were going to sneak out! You talked to half the hotel!"

"Of course I did. We were going shopping. Not escaping. We had to act the part," Louise said with a shrug. "It has to work. Who would think we'd be mail-order brides? We'll go, hide until things are sorted out, and leave. While I'm with that shopkeeper, I'm sure I'll be in a town large enough to wire Father's lawyer and see what I can find out. Maybe he can help us."

Mathilda still looked doubtful. Louise gave her a smile and squeezed her hand. "I'll see you soon on the ship. Trust me, Mattie. Nothing bad will happen. Besides, you wanted to go on the *Titanic*, didn't you?" With that, she left.

Louise wanted to look back and make sure Mathilda wasn't standing there, but she couldn't waste a moment. Crossing the street, she weaved her way through the crowd until she reached a department store. Once inside, she headed straight to the menswear.

"I need a man's shirt, suit, and trousers," she told the woman working there. "Also, that hat," she pointed. "They are to be a gift for my husband. We set sail on the *Titanic* today, so I've no time to get them made to order. The size doesn't have to be perfect. We can get it tailored on the ship, I'm sure. What do you have that's available now?"

The clerk helped her, and Louise also selected a small travel bag, paid in cash, took the packages, and set off toward the hotel again. Going up to her room, she was grateful the key she'd kept still worked. She dropped it on the mantle.

Quickly, Louise changed out of her dress and into the men's shirt, jacket, and trousers. Luckily, she had dark boots that would pass if no one stared at her small feet. Pulling her hair back tightly, she jammed the slightly too snug hat onto her head. If no one looked closely, she might just pull this off.

Hurriedly shoving her dress into the travel bag, she opened the hotel room door a crack, peeked to be sure no one was coming, and set off again to the hotel lobby, this time dressed as a man.

Under her arm she had a newspaper tucked, like many of the men she'd passed did. Hopefully she wouldn't run into Mr. Hillcock or Mr. Longsmith. She wasn't sure if they were still there or not, or how good her disguise was.

Louise had just gotten to the front of the hotel and past the doorman when she heard, "Mister! Hey, Mister!"

She froze as a meaty hand landed on her shoulder. Keeping her head low, she dropped her voice. "Eh?"

"Dropped your paper," the doorman said, offering it.

Louise took it, waved the paper in thanks, then spun away, walking quickly to lose herself in the crowd. It was only when she got away that she realized how incredibly sick she felt to her stomach. Still, the doorman hadn't recognized her as a woman, so she was off to a good start.

Now, to find the dock and Mathilda. Luckily, the dock wasn't too far away, and the crowd was quite heavy the nearer she drew.

"Excuse me, pardon me, beg pardon," Louise said in the deepest voice she could muster as she worked her way through the almost endless crowd. She'd never seen so many people before at once, and it felt a little overwhelming.

A nice, quiet, small town doesn't sound bad about now, she thought dryly. At least it would have some elbow room. As people jostled her on each side, one hand was kept on her hat, the other tightly around the handle of the bag.

At last, the *Titanic* loomed ahead. There was
no other word for it. The enormous ship seemed
to tower over everything. It truly was a marvel
of shipbuilding. Craning her neck back, Louise
forgot herself for a moment as she stared at it.
According to the newspaper, the ship's designer,
Thomas Andrews, would be on board as well.

Louise knew Mathilda would love to chat
with the man and learn every detail of *Titanic's*
wondrous design, and a pang of regret that they
must stay in the room and remain unseen for the
entire trip filled her. Still, there would be other
voyages and perhaps she and Mathilda could travel
on *Titanic* again one day and explore it fully.

Passengers were boarding, and Louise fumbled
for her ticket as she joined the line. There was chaos
as a woman's dog got loose. Louise concentrated on
keeping her head down the more people clustered
around her, but it was hard.

Pushed closer by the crowd that swept her along,
she let herself admire the graceful curves of the
ship and its endless portholes. She'd never seen
anything so large or magnificent. She wondered

what Mathilda thought. It was everything her sister had talked about, and then some.

Though the circumstances were not what she'd wanted, she hoped at least they'd have an enjoyable voyage. Even if they'd never left the stateroom.

"Deck D, sir," a steward said, glancing at her ticket.

Louise nodded and set off in the direction he pointed. She needed to move toward the protection of the interior—away from the deck and the chance of being seen from the dock. And she desperately hoped that Mr. Hillcock and Mr. Longsmith wouldn't be allowed to board without a ticket. Despite what she'd told Mathilda, she wasn't as confident as she pretended.

As Louise glanced once more at the ticket, she wondered if he really had bought these tickets, or if he'd come by them dishonestly. Was there a couple out there somewhere, disappointed they'd not be on the maiden voyage?

A flash of a familiar dress caught her eye, and she hurried to catch up. Without thinking, Louise reached out and grabbed her sister.

Mathilda turned, no recognition in her eyes, but fear filling them in an instant. Louise didn't understand why at first, then remembered she was dressed as a man, just as her sister struggled and opened her mouth to scream.

Chapter 6

Louise couldn't let Mathilda scream. It would bring everyone rushing over. She tightened her grip on her sister and hissed, "Mattie, it's me."

She raised her head briefly, just enough to let her sister see it was her, then lowered her head again, jamming the hat low. "Come on, into the room. Where is it?"

Mathilda led the way, glancing at the doors as they passed before stopping in front of one. With a nervous look behind her, Louise waited while Mathilda walked in, then followed close behind her. As soon as she was in the room, she locked the door behind them.

With a sigh of relief, Louise took off the men's hat and dropped it on one of the beds. She longed to change out of her ensemble, but wasn't sure if she could yet. It might not be safe to do so. She shrugged out of the jacket. The trousers were not uncomfortable, but they felt foreign.

Sensing Mathilda staring at her, she looked up. Her sister's face was one of absolute wonder.

"Louise, where on earth did you get that man's suit?"

"At a shop, of course," Louise answered. Sometimes her sister asked the strangest questions. Wasn't it an obvious answer? She shrugged. "Never mind about that. I—" at that moment, the incredible room caught her eye, and Louise turned slowly to take in the entire stateroom.

She had no idea a stateroom aboard a ship could be so luxurious. If this was second class, what kind of splendor was there in first class?

The room's walls were a glossy white paneling. They perfectly accented the floors, which were the newest and most expensive covering at the time, linoleum. A large sofa beckoned as a cozy area to read a book or sip tea, and the other furniture in the room was a mahogany wardrobe and small table, as well as a washbasin and mirror.

As Louise completed her examination of the room, her gaze settled on Mathilda. Her sister wore an expression of slight sadness. When their eyes met, Mathilda gave a small smile.

"Do you think perhaps we can dine in the dining room once? And perhaps walk along the promenade? Visit the baths?"

Louise's heart ached for her sister. They both knew they'd need to be confined to their room for the duration. She hated to have to say it aloud, though. Biting her lip, she gave a small nod. "I am sorry. Here, you get to have your dream travel experience, and it's less than favorable."

With a shake of her head, and a straightening of her shoulders, Mathilda said, "No, I'm here. I won't spoil what I can do by complaining."

Louise gave her sister a warm smile. That was typical of Mathilda. She always tried, and usually succeeded, in making the best out of each thing that came her way.

Mathilda continued, "The situation is too serious for it. Lou, what will we do if they come after us? And what kind of help do you think we can get from Father's lawyer?"

Louise didn't answer right away. She really didn't know, and it felt like it was all she'd been thinking about since she discovered the man she was to marry was likely a criminal. The few times she'd seen their father's lawyer hadn't been...pleasant. The man had talked over her, acting as though she didn't have a brain in her head, or the capability to understand more than the most simple of sentences. It irritated her.

Lost in her thoughts, it took Louise a moment to realize Mathilda was staring at her expectantly. With a small sigh, she said, "I'm not sure. I hope that they won't find us, but..." she stopped then, unable to finish her sentence. Louise turned toward one of her trunks.

How could she give her sister a false promise of safety? Still, they'd gotten this far. She was sure they'd make it the rest of the way. Her eyes darted to Mathilda, who was walking around the room exploring it.

I'm so sorry, Mattie. This is all my fault. Louise pressed her lips together as her eyes burned. *No tears. No more tears. Ever.*

As much as she longed to make a promise to Mathilda, there wasn't one she could give.

A sudden knock at the door startled her. She shoved her hat back on her head and stood as far away from the line of sight as possible.

Swallowing hard visibly, Mathilda opened the door just a crack. "May I help you?" she asked.

Tense, Louise waited to see who it was. "I just wanted to be sure you had everything, madam," a young male's voice said politely.

Her body unclenched. A steward. That was all. The roaring in her ears subsided, and she realized she missed the rest of the conversation.

"One problem solved," Mathilda said, after she closed the door. "He'll bring our meals," she said.

Louise nodded and removed the hat again. Opening her handbag, she pulled out the stack of papers she'd taken from Mr. Hillcock's bag. It was time to see what they were, and if they were worth keeping.

With the stack of papers in her lap, she sat on the sofa, examining them one by one.

"What are those?" Mathilda asked.

"I'm not sure," Louise confessed. She set the pile between them. "They were mixed in with the money I took from Mr. Hillcock's briefcase."

Sitting next to her on the sofa, Mathilda picked up a paper and looked at it carefully. "These look like promissory notes," she said after a moment.

Louise nodded. "I don't recognize any of the names, but look at these interest rates. It's…extortion, Mattie. Fifty percent interest on this one, forty here."

Her sister waved another. "This one here isn't even for money, it's for land."

"Yes, I see that. I thought I saw another one similar," Louise said. She shook her head slowly. The poor, desperate people who must have signed them. What a terrible thing.

Allowing herself to lean against the back of the sofa for just a moment, Louise looked up at the ceiling. "Either I've done something very foolish or I've saved us from something very foolish."

"If he wasn't a gangster, he was a crook," Mathilda said, and squeezed Louise's hand.

Absently, Louise nodded and straightened. She started to sort the papers into small piles. A familiar handwriting was on one, and she picked it up, peering a little closer.

Blinking several times, she shook her head slightly in disbelief. *This…can't be.*

Her hand trembled as she read the note, then read it again. The paper fluttered from her fingers onto the stateroom floor as the room started to spin.

How could Father do that?

Chapter 7

Mathilda's voice seemed to come from far away. Louise felt almost as if she were deep under water or fighting her way through an unpleasant dream. Everything seemed too slow, and though her sister's mouth was moving, she couldn't understand what she was saying.

Slumping against the sofa's back, Louise's mind tried to focus. It was difficult to form coherent thoughts.

Father's lawyer had sold them. He had sold her and Mattie. To criminals. Had Father known? He must have—his signature was there.

A cooling sensation on her temples and wrists brought her out of her fog. Mathilda was hovering with a damp cloth in her hand and a concerned look on her face. Struggling to sit up, Louise whispered, trying to explain, "The promissory note."

To her own ears, she sounded weak, faint, unwell. Judging by the alarm on Mathilda's face, it must have been true.

Mathilda picked the note up from the floor. She scanned it, then gasped, "We've been sold? Oh, Lou. What will we do? You can't go to Father's lawyer now. Mr. Brown sold us!"

Louise nodded, but she didn't answer. Summoning every ounce of determination and tensing her jaw, she went through the rest of the papers with shaking hands. There were no others with their names on it, just the one. Indeed, their father's lawyer had made out the note, but Father's signature was on it.

I give my daughters Louise and Mathilda Weston in exchange for the sum of fifteen thousand dollars.

The words seemed imprinted on her mind. A mixture of hurt, disgust, and anger filled her right now, as the initial shock faded.

Gathering the papers together in a stack, she frowned. What to do now? Even though she didn't recognize any of the other names, each of the notes must be incredibly important and obviously life changing to someone. Mr. Longsmith was described as a con man and blackmailer in the newspaper, perhaps these people were being blackmailed or forced to sign away something precious to them against their will.

Had that been the case with Mr. Brown and their father? Or had he sold them knowingly?

"I thought he was a friend to Father," Mathilda said.

Louise's heart ached at the catch in her little sister's throat. And the thought that perhaps she'd caused this hurt somehow.

Straightening her spine, she gave her sister a reassuring look, and spoke in her best no-nonsense voice. "We don't know the whole story. But until then, we must keep these papers safe." Standing, she moved to one of her trunks and pulled out a small book that had a ribbon tied around it.

"*A Lady's Book of Poetry?*" Mathilda asked.

Louise didn't answer. Her sister would see soon enough and save her the time of the explanation. As the book cover opened, Louise flipped through the first few pages and revealed a hollow. About a year before, she'd cut apart the book to create a secret space, thinking no one would want to open such a book, and therefore not suspect its true purpose.

"How clever," Mathilda breathed.

Louise's cheeks flushed at her sister's praise.

"Louise, what made you think of that? I must make one for myself."

Proudly, Louise answered, "You learn a few things in boarding school that governesses don't teach." She recalled her first week there when one of the older girls had shown the newer girls this trick.

Back then, sweets or pocket money or even love notes smuggled in by local boys had hidden in the hollow—anything one didn't want the headmistress to find. Louise had done it herself several times over the years. This time, she finally had something more important than a few trinkets to go inside of the hiding area.

Making the papers into a neat bundle, Louise folded them and placed them in the hollow. Quickly, she retied the ribbon around the book and placed it back in her handbag.

Looking at her sister, Louise warned in a low voice, "This must never be left alone. I'm not sure what I will do, but it shall be our insurance. For now, forget what you saw. You'll go west, as will I, but I will be looking for someone to help. I'm sure I'll be able to figure out something."

Mathilda nodded and turned away. Louise suppressed a sigh. She knew her sister was worried and wished she had words to ease her mind.

Actually, Louise wished someone had the words to calm and reassure *her*.

This had become far more serious than she thought it would be. This wasn't running away from an unwanted marriage, but from someone who would bring them back at all costs, now that they had these notes and the knowledge of who the men were. There was no way at all that Mr. Hillcock and Mr. Longsmith wouldn't suspect them of having possession of the papers. It was only a matter of time before they were caught.

★★★

Over the next four days, they remained in their room, quietly passing time. If they weren't reading, they played cards and talked softly. A steward served meals to the stateroom, and they took turns using the washroom down the corridor. Louise's handbag was kept safe at all times, and never out of sight. When she went to wash, Mathilda wore it around her wrist until Louise returned, who then wrapped it around hers.

They were taking no chances at all with this precious and dangerous information.

Despite the constant worry and tension that seemed to fill the air every waking moment, there were times they found they could enjoy themselves onboard the *Titanic*. The second night there, Mathilda discovered that there were few people about on the small bit of promenade nearby them. After a bit of reluctance, Louise gave in to her sister's pleading, and they went out.

Admittedly, she did enjoy both the change of scenery and the fresh air. Louise could also tell how much it both relaxed and invigorated her younger sister. Though she'd not complained, Mathilda had been full of questions, wondering what other parts of the ship looked like and restless, as the small room, though well made, did get tiresome to be confined in.

That night as they stood looking over the water, it was frigid. There was no other way to put it. Thin streams of vapor came from Louise's nostrils as she breathed out, and for a moment, she allowed herself the whimsey of imagining she was the mythical being from her favorite childhood fairy tale, puffing out smoke as she flew over a village.

"Look how dark it is," Mathilda breathed in wonder, her hands resting on the rail. "It's so cold, too."

"Mm," Louise agreed, snapping out of her imagination and wrapping her coat tighter. The chill seemed to penetrate through the cloth. "I'll bet the water is quite icy."

"I'm grateful to be here, well away from it," Mathilda sighed. "I never thought I'd say it, but I'll be glad to get on land. Being out here with nothing but water around makes me feel uncomfortable in a way I never could have imagined."

Now that her sister said something, that incredible vastness made her uncomfortable too. Suddenly, their room seemed very appealing, and Louise pretended to yawn. "I agree. Let's go back. I'm tired and it's after midnight."

The two made their way to the stateroom and readied for bed. As she had the other nights, Louise placed her handbag underneath her pillow and lay there, one hand on it.

Though the pillow was soft and with the late hour, she should have been tired, but Louise's mind wouldn't calm. She wondered what waited for her and Mathilda once they docked. Would Mr. Hillcock suspect they were on the ship? Would he be there waiting? Or could they manage to get a train to take them west before he realized they were back in the United States?

That question opened up a whole new Pandora's box. What would the man she was running to be like? Would her sister get a kind man? What would it be like living so far away from everything and everyone she'd ever known, and as a wife?

Though she worried about this, deep inside she knew it didn't matter what happened. There was no other choice. How could she do anything less with the terrible shock of Mr. Hillcock and his associate, and now their father's lawyer?

Finally, Louise drifted to sleep, only to be woken by a sudden and frantic banging on the door.

Trading a glance with Mathilda, they went to the door together. It wasn't until they opened it, Louise realized she was dressed as a woman, not a man. It was too late now, though.

A steward they'd not seen before looked at them urgently. Beyond him, people were quickly leaving their rooms, pulling on jackets and flotation devices.

"You need to get a life jacket on and come to the main deck," he told them calmly, but forcefully.

"But why?" Louise asked.

There was no answer. The man's eyes held a worry, and a muscle in his cheek twitched. The sisters glanced at each other and then back at the steward, who had moved down the hall and was knocking at another door.

A woman rushed past them, and Louise called out to her, "Please! What is the matter?"

The woman turned and laughed, "Why, we've struck an iceberg. Isn't that incredible? They are loading the lifeboats with women and children, just to be careful, you understand." She turned away again, calling to a friend a few paces away. "I've got it, dear. We can go now."

"But the boat is unsinkable," Mathilda said, her voice filled with surprise. "Why would they load the women and children?"

Louise shrugged. "I don't know. But that's how I shall dress. As a woman. I won't let the proof of what's happened to us risk not getting to the authorities. Hurry."

Pulling on a dress and snatching up her coat and handbag, Louise waited for Mathilda to do the same. Her sister was only a few breaths slower than she was. Opening the door, several inches of water now stood sloshing about their ankles and filling their room as they left.

"I'm sure we'll be back soon," Louise said uneasily as they made their way to the upper deck. Her shoes were drenched, and she wondered how she'd get them dry. There was a large creaking sound and the water's speed as it rose increased. Louise glanced over her shoulder, swallowed hard, and moved faster.

Mathilda said something, but it was lost as they rounded a corner and it grew nosier.

Around them, on the upper deck, passengers stood. Some were holding glasses of something steaming or bubbly, clustered together talking. A few young men had found a chunk of ice, and were kicking it back and forth, laughing. A large number stood at the railing, pointing in the distance.

"Why do they not go?" Mathilda whispered to her sister. Her eyes were wide.

Louise wondered the same as a feeling of panic filled her, but she shrugged. It was important to stay calm. "Because it's just a precaution. This boat cannot sink. But," she added firmly, "it is a precaution we will take. We have not made it this far to not take every opportunity afforded."

As the crowd began to swell, she felt for her sister's hand. She must get Mattie to a lifeboat. Whether something happened or not, it was her responsibility to keep her sister safe. "Stay close," she warned.

A crewman was loading a boat a short distance away and Louise hurried toward him. The crewman was waving his arm and the lifeboat started to lower. There were not many women within it. It was perhaps a third full.

"Wait!" Louise called as loudly as she could. "Please wait!" She waved her free hand. The crewman saw her.

"Hold!" the crewman shouted to the lifeboat, then turned to Mathilda and Louise. "Would you ladies like in?"

"Please," Louise said. She felt nervous, thinking about being in the dark waters on such a small craft, but pushed the feeling aside. With a smile, she continued, "We shall enjoy the view of the ship from a different perspective until we are allowed to board again."

With a nod, the crewman helped Mathilda in first, then her. The sisters sat next to each other. A few more people climbed in after them and the crewman called out for more passengers. None answered his call, and the boat lowered, about half full. Two crewmen were at the oars, and the boat set out a short distance from the *Titanic*.

Much as it had been only a short time before when she and Mathilda were on the promenade, the moonless night was clear and crisp. To see the *Titanic* from his angle was impressive. The massive ship was lit, alive with people and music, and laughter. It was a sharp contrast from their small craft. In the calm water, with only gentle waves lapping at their lifeboat as music, her passengers silent, and a dim light from a small lantern casting a soft glow, it felt strange. And small. Yes, Louise thought, so very small and insignificant in comparison to the enormous ship before them.

If something were to happen, how long could we stay on this lifeboat? And how would anyone know to rescue us?

Mathilda's frightened voice broke through her thoughts, and Louise looked at her sharply, then toward her sister's pointing finger.

"The...the ship. It's listing. The *Titanic* is sinking."

Chapter 8

Louise laughed softly. The sound seemed to carry in the still night. She reached to comfort her sister and took her hand. "Nonsense. Why, you are just tired, dear. See? It's—"

But she stopped. Mathilda was correct. The powerful ship was tilted, slanting. One half raised as the other sank, dropping lower into the dark waters.

But how could this be? Unsinkable, they'd said! Her fingers tightened around her handbag and she hardly breathed as she watched the ship.

On board, the small figures she knew were humans began to run, frantically. They moved toward the side that was raising, perhaps to balance it? It was impossible. Filling with water, the ship was heavy and starting to sink. There was no way anyone could deny it now. As she watched, she knew there was also no way to stop it. Anything done, would be futile.

The woman in front of her drew her collar closer, and as she spoke, vapor came out in little puffs. "No need to worry," she said. "There's a ship nearby, I suspect. If anything were to happen, they'd come for us."

It surprised Louise how the woman seemed so calm. Did she not see the *Titanic* sinking? As she glanced around the lifeboat, Louise observed the others on board seemed that way as well. Some were talking quietly, one was digging through her handbag, and a few were even dozing. They didn't seem at all aware of the danger the hundreds and hundreds of others on board the *Titanic* were in.

Louise and Mathilda watched as lifeboats were packed, then lowered. But there weren't enough. Even from this distance, she could see that. Figures ran around, and it was near chaos. Louise watched, holding her breath and praying, but she didn't see more lifeboats releasing. There were still so many on board. She glanced to Mathilda, who was watching with horror on her face, the very same thing Louise felt.

Suddenly, at a speed which surprised her, the tremendous ship slid backward into the water, almost as though it were being pulled down. With a terrific groan that filled the night, the ship snapped almost in half.

"Will it float?" Louise gasped. She didn't expect an answer, but she hoped one of the crewmen would know. They didn't answer, though. Their heads were also pointed in the direction of the tragedy.

"Dear God! Save them," a woman shouted, her cry rattling the others aboard the lifeboat. The other passengers now no longer seemed calm. Someone started crying, then another joined in.

In the distance, the small figures on the deck of *Titanic* began to fall into the water, first one or two at a time, then many. Some jumped, some were flung. Either way, Louise knew each passenger would meet the icy and unforgiving ocean's waters. The chances of surviving would be slim.

Their lifeboat swayed dangerously and she grabbed on to Mathilda to steady herself. "We must help," a woman screamed as she lunged for an oar. "My husband!"

She was pulled back by another woman who tried to soothe her. The woman was frantic, trying to get away. The boat swayed.

One of the crewmen shook his head. "We stay," he said firmly, "else we will be overrun. My duty is to the protection of you ladies."

In the distance, the sickening sounds of splashing and shouting faded all too quickly as the icy Atlantic claimed both the unsinkable ship and those aboard.

God have mercy on them. Please let their deaths have been swift and painless.

A woman began to say the Lord's Prayer, and everyone in the boat recited it with her. Louise shivered nearly uncontrollably. From terror or cold, she wasn't sure. Her eyes couldn't seem to leave the small dots in the distance she knew were the men and women and—God forbid—children of the *Titanic*, now taking their final rest.

Every discomfort she had felt over the last four days, including her current cold, wet feet, seemed so insignificant in comparison. Louise felt selfish. How many had perished? There were titans of industry aboard. How would the nation suffer for their loss? How many families were now missing loved ones, perhaps never to have the comfort of knowing if their final moments were peaceful?

She realized she was still squeezing Mathilda's hand and released it, turning to look at her sister. Mathilda's cheeks glistened with wetness. Tears.

Seeing her sister staring at her, Mathilda spoke hoarsely, "I will never get on the water again."

"Nor I," Louise replied, and wrapped her arms around her sister.

Time passed slowly. There was no way of telling how long they bobbed on the water. There were faint hiccupping sobs from the women around them. After what seemed hours, small, dark shapes grew larger, and other lifeboats, each with their pinpricks of light, began to gather. Louise's boat slowly rowed toward a cluster of other boats forming.

Off in the distance, a large shadow filled with tiny lights appeared on the horizon. "A ship," one woman to Louise's rear gasped, pointing.

"We're saved," another cried, and half rose.

"Hold," a crewman warned. "No sudden movements. We don't want to capsize."

The women obeyed and sat motionless. Everyone's focus was on one thought.

Survival.

Soon, their lifeboat joined another, and another, forming a small floating island as the lifeboats connected. Before long, the shadow in the distance grew close, and it was a ship.

Rescue had come. Louise felt a great relief. Things happened so quickly, she moved through in a daze. There was shouting, and more tears, and a few hugs. The surviving *Titanic* passengers were helped onboard the *RMS Carpathia*, given thick blankets to wrap around themselves and mugs of steaming tea. The *Carpathia's* passengers assisted as much as they could by giving up their own personal belongings, such as warm, dry socks and beds, though there were heartaches that would never heal.

As Mathilda sat huddled against Louise on *Carpathia's* deck, she whispered, "Do you know, Lou, I think perhaps I shall be glad to marry a man from a small town. It sounds quite dull, and after today, that is what I long for."

Winding her arm around to pull her sister closer, Louise laughed. It was bitter, she could tell, but it was filled with agreement. Each time she closed her eyes, the horrific scene replayed in her mind.

"The truth is, I'd prefer to be doing sums right now myself, totaling up a customer's purchase of sugar and flour."

A uniformed officer of their rescue ship stooped near them. In one hand he clutched a pencil, the other held a notebook. "Names, misses?"

Louise opened her mouth, but Mathilda answered instead. "Mathilda and Louise Weston."

He moved away and Louise pulled back from her sister, angrily hissing, "Why did you say that?" There was a lot more she wanted to say, but she didn't. Not in public. And also because she was a lady.

The realization of what she'd told the officer flashed over Mathilda's face, and her face grew white. "I wasn't thinking." She looked around wildly. "Where did he go? Perhaps I can stop him."

Trying to keep her tone calm and not draw more attention to them, Louise put her hand on her sister's arm to stop her. "There's no point. Others overheard you. It's such a large disaster, the survivor names are sure to be printed in the paper."

Another unwelcome complication. This might have worked in their favor…but not now.

Had the dangerous escape been for nothing? Louise knew it had been an accident, a tired slip of the tongue, but Mathilda had possibly led their pursuers right to them.

Chapter 9

Louise stepped off the *Carpathia*, Mathilda by her side. Exhausted, they propelled themselves forward, with the pressing need to hide. Louise was immensely grateful to have land beneath their feet again, and judging by Mathilda's contented sigh, she was as well.

A crowd stood, watching the passengers disembark. There were quiet murmurs, many people craning necks, and a few shouts of a name, but for the most part, a solemn mood was amongst the crowd.

Wasting no time, Louise took her sister's arm, lest they get separated in the crowd that was now pushing them along. "We need to find transportation," she said, standing on her toes and trying to see over the heads of the people in front of her.

A man in a dock worker's uniform overhead her. "To your left at the end, miss," he said. "Cabs to anywhere you need."

Louise gave him a smile. "Thank you."

She and Mathilda hurried their way to a carriage, where a driver sat waiting with his horse. "Misses," he said, doffing his cap to them.

"Penn Station, please," Louise said as Mathilda climbed into the carriage and slid across to the far side. Her sister in, she climbed behind her and shut the door.

"You got it," the driver said, and set off at a quick pace.

Louise leaned close to her sister. Though the horse's hooves were a good barrier to her voice, she didn't wish to be overheard. "We will buy tickets without delay," Louise said. "I was looking at the map and we can travel most of the way together."

Her sister leaned against the seat and nodded. "That will be good."

"I think that—" Before she could say anything else, they arrived at the station. Louise paid the driver, and she and Mathilda hurried in. Approaching a ticket counter, Louise pulled her hat low, stated their destinations, and slid some money across to the seller.

Mathilda had been waiting a few steps away.

"It departs in just a moment," Louise said, somewhat breathlessly. "Hurry." She pointed to a distant platform.

"How fortunate they are boarding right away," Mathilda said, taking long steps to keep up.

"I agree. The sooner we are on the move, the better," Louise said. "Go on, I'll catch up."

She stopped at a young boy selling papers. "One please," she said, handing him some coins.

Tucking the paper under her arm, she scurried to catch up to Mathilda. They climbed the steps to the train car and found an empty compartment. Louise opened the paper. Mathilda sat next to her, reading as well.

Obviously, the *Titanic* sinking was on the front page. What she was looking for, praying against, was the list of survivors that were sure to be listed. Finding the list, they scanned it, hoping desperately not to see their names. But there they were, in black and white: Louise and Mathilda Weston.

Mathilda looked at her with mournful eyes, but Louise simply squeezed her sister's hand and closed the paper. Then she leaned against the seat and closed her eyes. Louise wasn't tired, but she wanted to think.

They weren't far now from being separated. For the first time in years, she wouldn't have Matilda, and perhaps more importantly, Mathilda wouldn't have her.

Opening her eyes, she shot a glance at her younger sister. Mathilda had also closed her eyes, and her head was resting against the window. Mattie was so inexperienced in the world, Louise worried about her, but there was no way the two of them could go on together. Besides the obvious of it being easier to find two women on the run than one, that's not how being a mail-order bride worked.

Her mind replayed the last few weeks, searching for some clue as to how to make things right. She was tired of asking herself that question. When would things just go well for once? Allowing herself a moment of self pity, Louise sighed and stared out the window, letting her mind blank. The soothing motion of the train made her yawn. Then yawn again.

"Next stop, Midway!" a man called, rapping on the window of their compartment.

Louise startled. She must have dozed off. "Mattie," she said. "That's you, dear. Midway. I switch and travel on to Richmond."

Mathilda's lips trembled, and her eyes filled with tears. One slipped down her cheek as she threw herself at Louise with a sob.

Holding in her own reaction, Louise and Mathilda embraced, and she tried to soothe her younger sister. In her arms, Louise could feel Mathilda shaking. Though her throat was tight and her eyes burned with unshed tears, she managed to choke out, "This isn't goodbye. It's see you soon.

You'll have a new name, as will I, and we will be safe. Then we'll reunite."

"But how will I find you?" Mathilda asked, still clinging to her. Her voice was muffled, as her head was buried into Louise.

The train slowed. Reluctantly, Louise pulled back and shook her head. "I don't know yet. But we will. Keep the receipt for where you sent the telegram. That gives you a starting point." Leaning close, she kissed Mathilda's forehead, then gave her a smile and a little push to the door. "Hurry, my dear Mattie."

Mathilda exited and turned, waving goodbye as the train moved on without her. Louise watched until she could no longer see her, and then she broke the promise to herself and let her tears fall. A moment later, she wiped them away, took a deep breath, and straightened her shoulders. It wouldn't be much longer before she'd be arriving herself.

Soon, she'd be known as Mrs…whatever. She wasn't sure, really. She just knew it wouldn't be Mrs. Hillcock, and she was grateful for that.

In what seemed like no time at all, the train slowed, then stopped, and Louise gathered her confidence, raised her chin, and strode off the train.

It was time to meet her destiny head on.

Chapter 10

Biting her lip, Louise tried to calm the nervousness in her stomach. She wasn't really sure where she should go. Admittedly, she didn't even know who she was looking for. Hopefully, some other woman hadn't taken her place.

Eyeing the town around her, she searched for the telegram office. They, or the post office, would possibly know where she needed to go. Two-story buildings, with large false fronts rising much higher, greeted her. Signs were hand painted, but done well, and the rail station's large clock next to her was simple, but with large numbers and hands so the time could be seen from a far distance.

Stepping forward briskly, she headed in the direction of what she assumed was the center of the town, also hoping there was a decent dress shop.

"Miss?"

A little girl about six or seven with two blonde braids stood, holding a bundle of wildflowers and staring at her hesitantly.

"Me?" Louise asked, looking around to see if she was talking to someone else.

The girl nodded. She bit her lip and squeezed the flowers tightly in her fist.

Louise knelt down. "What is it, my dear? Are you looking for someone?" She gave a small laugh and a shrug, but spoke kindly. "I admit, I might not be the best person to help with that, having just arrived, but I shall, if I can."

"Are you Miss Louise?" the girl asked.

Louise sat back on her heels. "Why, yes, I am."

"I'm Ellie," the girl said. "I think you're supposed to be my new ma." She thrust the slightly bruised flowers at Louise.

"Why, thank you," Louise said, a little surprised, and she reached to take them. Ellie was not what she'd expected, and she was sweet and polite. Things seemed off to a good start.

She held the crushed bouquet to her nose and breathed in deeply. The little girl was watching, her eyes wide and hopeful. "They are quite lovely, Ellie. Did you pick them?"

Ellie's face lit and she nodded. "I did. Pa sent me here for you. We didn't know what day you were coming, so every day I picked some new ones and waited."

"Oh, my dear," Louise said. "I am so sorry you've waited. I had a…bit of an accident on the way here, so I was delayed."

"Do you have any more bags?" Ellie asked. "Pa said to get him and he'd carry them."

"I don't, dear. That was the accident. All my luggage was lost."

"Good thing we own a store," Ellie said. "Maybe we have some of what you need." She reached up and shyly took Louise's hand.

Smiling down, Louise followed the little girl a short distance down the street. They went to the shop that had a sign declaring *Richmond General Store*.

Louise was delighted to see through the window the store was well stocked, and quite large. Perhaps the man she was to marry would be a little more well off than she'd imagined. Her eyes swept the store as they entered, taking in barrels and jars, not missing the fact it was a little disorderly. She could feel useful here, setting things to right.

"Pa!" Ellie called out, "Pa! She's here!"

A little boy of perhaps two came rushing out from behind a counter and gaped at her. By the shock of white blond hair, Louise was sure he was Ellie's sister. But she had thought there was only to be one child? Before she could tell him hello, a tall and incredibly good looking man came from the other direction.

"Hello," he said, his voice a rich timbre. "I'm Jake Smith. You must be Louise."

For a moment, Louise forgot how to talk, she was so stunned. Before her stood a man who looked like he'd walked right out of a novel. With dark hair and smiling eyes, he was devastatingly dashing. There was no other word for it. His white shirtsleeves were rolled up, showing muscles that made her want to reach out and touch them.

There was a thumping sound, and it took Louise a moment to realize it was the sound of her heart. She stammered, "Ah, a.."

"Pa—" Ellie, God bless her, interrupted, "Miss Louise had an accident. All her bags are gone."

"Is that so?" Jake turned his eyes toward Louise. Still feeling flustered, she simply nodded.

"Well, you are welcome to what we have here in the shop," he offered. Moving to the front window, he pointed across the street. "Right there across from us is the dressmaker. She does a fine job. Get what you need. I'll pay for it."

"Oh," Louise said, having finally found her tongue. "That's not necessary, really. I have my own money to help at first, but I do appreciate the offer."

"It's not an offer," Jake replied. "You are going to be my wife and their mother. What kind of a man would I be if I let you pay for your own dresses? Ellie," he addressed the little girl, "would you watch the shop while I show your new Ma where her room will be until we get married? Then maybe you'd like to go with her to order some dresses?"

With a proud nod, Ellie climbed onto a tall stool. Her brother climbed up next to her onto a box and they both sat, drawing on a slate.

"They are adorable," Louise said as she followed Jake to the back of the store and a flight of stairs. "With that fair hair, they must have taken after their mother? But I thought your advertisement said only one child?"

"Must have been a misprint," Jake said. "I hope that won't be a problem for you. They've been in sore need of a woman around," he continued, glancing at her while walking up the steps. "Their ma died just after Phil, that's the boy, was born. Been us ever since, but though I can cook and clean, I'm no substitute for the love and care of a mother. It's also hard running the store and caring for them at the same time. Gotten to a point I need help."

Louise followed, and when they reached the top of the stairs, she said, "It's not a problem. Truly,

I understand. My own mother passed away when my younger sister was still quite young. I became her mother, and I'm happy to do the same for Ellie and Phil, giving them all the love I can."

Jake searched her face and nodded. "I think you will," he said slowly. He moved toward a closed door. "It was a bit of a surprise to us, you writing and saying you were on the way. The preacher's out of town for another week or so, and so until he's back, you'll stay here."

He swung the door open, showing a small and tidy room. A single bed was pushed against the wall, and a small chest of drawers was on the other side. The room was plain, there was no personalization at all, but Louise was relieved to see it was clean. She set the small bundle of flowers from Ellie on top of the chest of drawers.

"Thank you," she said.

Jake nodded and moved back toward the stairs. He looked at her, then away, then back at her again. "Miss…" his voice trailed off.

"Louise is fine," she said, not wanting to give her last name unless she had to.

He nodded. "Louise, these children are dear to me. I also trust their instincts. As much as I need a mother for them, and you must need a marriage since you are here, I want you to know that until the preacher comes, you're on a kind of probation."

"Probation?" Louise asked, raising her eyebrows in surprise. *Did people do that?*

"That's right." Jake rubbed at the back of his head. "I need someone to care for them in case…" He stopped. "I need someone to care for them and love them."

"What about you?" Louise asked, curious about his comment. "You don't want a bride for…" her cheeks blazed and she glanced at her shoes.

There was a long silence and when she looked up, she was surprised to see Jake's face was also heated. "I do want a bride," he said, "but seeing those children are cared for is my first concern."

"That's very thoughtful and wonderful of you," Louise said.

"No," Jake said, and his face darkened. "It's the right thing to do, because I've been selfish. I'm trying to make amends before it's too late."

Chapter 11

Now it was Louise's turn to search his face. "Selfish?" she asked. She could tell that Jake was struggling with wanting to say something, but he was preventing himself. Finally, he answered.

"We all have secrets," he said with a tight smile. "It's my experience that some mail-order brides have them as well."

Louise sucked in her breath. Did he know? He didn't seem to see her response though, as he continued, "I don't know a lot about you yet, Miss...Louise. But I can tell you are a good woman."

He turned and went down the stairs. Blinking a few times, Louise followed, a bit unsure what to make of the strange interaction. While it was true, she hadn't known what to expect, a man with secrets of his own was unexpected.

Ellie and Phil were still at the counter and both sprang up as she walked in. "Can we go now, Pa?" Ellie asked eagerly.

"Yep," Jake said. "Phil, you've got to stay and help me count apples. And eat them. Can't sell something that doesn't taste good."

"Can't sell," Phil repeated, and shook his head solemnly, following his father over to the apple display. Louise smiled at their backs, and followed Ellie across the street, her handbag tight in her grip.

The people who went past didn't look at her, a thing which relieved Louise. The town felt peaceful. She was looking forward to that.

A small chime tinkled as Ellie pushed open the door, and when an older woman with glasses came out from a back room, Ellie burst, "This is gonna be my new ma, Miss Winston. She needs some dresses."

Louise laughed in slight embarrassment. "Yes. Thank you for the introduction, Ellie." She turned to Miss Winston. "I do need dresses, and as soon as you can make them. I'm afraid I've only this dress and one more. There was an accident with my luggage, and none will be recovered."

The other woman nodded, already moving around her with a tape measurer and notepad. "Mmhmm," she said, writing down measurements. "What do you like?"

Louise started to answer, then stopped. "How much are your dresses?" she asked.

"Pa said put them on his account," Ellie spoke up.

"Yes, dear, but I can pay for these," Louise said. "We aren't married yet."

Ellie's face scrunched, and she waited while Louise and Miss Winston talked and looked at fabric. A short time later, Louise and Ellie left, with promise of new dresses as soon as possible.

Louise had chosen four, with two to be simple and suitable for working in the shop in pale pink and lilac colors, one in cream with lace at the throat and sleeves, and a final one that was much more elegant, with a deep blue silk that played beautifully to her complexion. She wasn't sure there would be a need for such a thing here, but when she'd seen the fabric, she knew she must have a dress made of it.

"When you and Pa get married, I have a new dress to wear," Ellie said happily. "Miss Winston made it for me."

"I should like to see it," Louise said, as they walked into the store.

At the front counter, Phil was eating an apple while Jake was helping a customer. Louise waited quietly until the store was empty again, then asked, "I know you also wanted help in the store. So, how can I help?"

Jake looked up from a ledger book and asked, "Can you do sums? I'm a little behind on this thing." He motioned to the page.

"Of course," she said, and took up a pencil. "I'll have it current for you quite soon."

"Great," Jake answered, relief in his voice.

"Almost Ma," Ellie asked, coming up and tugging on her skirt.

Louise hid her smile at the name. "Yes, Ellie?"

"What do you cook?"

That was a good question. What did she cook? Not much was the answer. Soups and stews? She was passable. Bread? Well, more like bricks. Her cookies and cakes could stop a hammer, and—

"Now, Ellie, you can't be tired of my food already?" Jake said teasingly.

"No, I like your cooking. I just wondered what she makes," Ellie said.

"Ah, well," Louise said, "the truth is, I'm…" How to say it? Could she word it so that she didn't sound like a terrible cook? "…a bit out of practice on many things. I lived with my sister for quite a while, and she did most of the cooking. I did breakfasts, and she did dinners."

"I like flapjacks," Phil said, through a mouthful of apple.

"That's my specialty," Louise smiled at him.

"Flapjacks for dinner?" Ellie asked. Her eyes grew wide. "Can we, Pa?"

Jake laughed. "Louise just got here. It's her first night. How about I cook, and after she's settled in, she can make you some flapjacks?"

Both children nodded, and Jake winked at her over their heads. Louise smiled, and then realized it was a genuine smile. Not something she'd done much of lately. Jake Smith was certainly very different from Mr. Hillcock. She liked him a great deal more. It seemed he was the type of person you could talk to, laugh with, and smile at. It was comfortable being around him, and it was obvious the children adored him.

As Louise worked on the store ledger, she couldn't help but think how so far, it was quite different from what she'd imagined, and it wasn't entirely unpleasant. In fact, she was rather enjoying herself, despite the situation she was in.

She only hoped Mathilda was doing well. As the children's laughter at a rolling toy that wobbled along the shop floor made her look up, another thought came to her. She also hoped that neither of them had brought trouble hot on their heels to the innocents they were with.

Chapter 12

Louise stood in front of the stove. It was time. She could do this. Ellie sat in the corner of the kitchen, her head overtop a children's storybook, looking at the pictures.

Pressing her lips together, Louise put her hands on her hips and nodded. Then she pushed up her sleeves and started to add flour to a bowl. Then lard, salt, and baking powder. She mixed it together. It was still crumbly. Frowning at the mess, she remembered. Milk and water. Splashing the liquid a little at a time, she beat it with a wooden spoon.

The unappetizing mixture was lumpy and sticky. Dumping it out onto the counter, she tried to form biscuits. It wasn't working. The dough covered her hands and made stringy, gloopy, blobs. With a grunt, she dropped them on the baking sheet anyway. Drop biscuits. That's what she'd call them. Jake wouldn't know they weren't the style back east.

Wiping her hands off, she checked on her stew bubbling on the stove. That, at least, looked right. Thankfully, stews and soups were easy. Dump it all in a pot, stir, and add some salt and pepper until it tasted good.

She poked at the blobs on the baking sheet and slid them into the oven. Jake had a fine stove. Mathilda would have been drooling over it. Not that her sister was too much better of a cook, but at least she knew how to make more than stew and flapjacks. It seemed the better one's cooking device, the easier it should be to produce something tasty, but Louise didn't see that as the case for her.

That morning, she'd made Jake and the children breakfast. It had gone over well. Flapjacks always did. How many more times could she make them before everyone was sick of them? That was the real question.

Lunch was always a cold lunch, and there were enough leftovers from the night before that she hadn't had to worry about it. Jake had shown her around the shop, and she familiarized herself with it, the catalogue used when they specially ordered, and the customers who came in.

Stirring the stew once more, she set the ladle aside and turned to Ellie. "How is the book?" she asked.

"I don't know," Ellie said. "I can't read yet."

Louise was about to offer to read the story to her when Ellie closed the book, looked up at her with big eyes, and asked, "Will you tell me what mothers do?"

The question caught Louise off guard, but she sat across from Ellie and smiled. "That's a very big question. What is it you want to know?"

Ellie looked down at the table. She was silent for so long, Louise wasn't sure she'd heard the question. Then she noticed little splashes as tears struck the tabletop.

"You seem sad," Louise said softly. "Do you want to tell me why?"

"It's cause when Molly Jefferson came in the store with her ma, she told me that getting a new one doesn't mean I really have a ma. It just means Pa gets a wife."

Louise sat back. "I see," she said. "And so you want to know if that's true?"

"I want to know what a ma does," Ellie said again. "Then maybe if you do those things, then I'll know you are my ma for real, and you'll stay and not leave like my last ma."

Sucking in a breath, Louise was heartbroken by the little girl's expression. It was a mixture of matter-of-fact and sadness. Closing her eyes for a brief moment, she remembered the loss of her own mother, and how she and Mathilda had felt so lost and empty, unsure what to do. To be so young, and to have a new mother suddenly…what was that like? How difficult this must be for Ellie as well.

Louise pulled her chair close to Ellie and wrapped an arm around her. The little girl snuggled close. "Well, I don't know very much about your ma," she began, "but I do know she must have loved you very much."

Ellie sniffled, but didn't say anything.

"I lost my ma too," Louise said.

Looking up at her, Ellie sniffled again. "What happened?"

"I don't quite know," Louise said. "I was away at finishing school. That's where some young ladies go to learn different things. My younger sister, Mathilda, was too young to go, so she had a governess. That's a teacher who lives at your house."

"Wow," Ellie said. "You must have been rich."

"We were," Louise agreed. "Until my mother had her accident. She was riding on her horse and the horse startled. She fell from it. The doctors tried to help her, but they couldn't."

"Like my ma!" Ellie said, straightening up. "When she got sick, the doctors couldn't help her either."

"That's right," Louise agreed. "Well, then it was just my sister, me, and our father. But he was so heartbroken, he died a little while later too."

Ellie snuggled into Louise's arms. "If Pa dies, Phil and I will be all alone," she said. "You have to stay, Almost Ma."

Louise laughed. "What a funny name you've given me."

"It's because you aren't my ma yet," Ellie told her, her young face serious. "But I can't wait to call you ma. Isn't polite to call grownups by their first name, Pa says. But what about you? What things did your ma do?"

Understanding the question now, Louise nodded. It was obvious that Ellie wasn't sure her place, and she wasn't sure what mothers did, and if it would be things that she liked, because she'd been so long without one. It was a feeling she understood well. At the moment, she wasn't quite sure of her place, either.

Clearing her throat, Louise answered, "Well, while each mother is different, generally they take care of their children. They teach them things, like how to tie their shoes, and how to sing songs. Mothers tell stories, and give hugs and kisses, and when a child gets hurt, they try and make them feel better."

"What about cooking?" Ellie asked.

Louise winced. "Yes, some mothers teach their children how to cook. I'm not sure that will be me. If you'll keep my secret, Ellie, I'll be honest with you, I'm not a very good cook."

Ellie grinned up at her, all traces of tears gone. "What are you best at?" she asked.

"Stories," Louise said, taking up the picture book. "I am fabulous at telling stories."

Opening the cover, she started to read to Ellie. Forgetting herself, Louise acted out the parts to the child's delight. She'd just spun around, shouting, "I'll get you, you evildoer!" when she crashed into someone. Looking up, her face colored as she saw it was Jake, who had Phil in one arm and a huge grin on his face.

"Almost Ma was reading!" Ellie shouted. "Don't stop!"

"Yes," Jake said, letting his eyes wander over Louise. "Don't stop."

Suddenly conscious of her messy hair and apron, Louise cleared her throat. She turned away from him. She was on the final page. It wouldn't be fair to Ellie to not finish properly. Taking a deep breath, she resumed her role as the hero. "And taking his longbow, Robin Hood shot the arrow and saved the beautiful princess. The end."

Applause filled the kitchen. So did a burning smell. "Oh no!" Louise cried, dropping the book on the table and rushing to the oven. Pulling out the biscuits, she stared at the darkened lumps.

Ellie's serious eyes met hers, and then Louise looked at Jake. He stood next to her and poked at one of the biscuits. "Looks flavorful," he said, his tone neutral, but his eyes filled with humor.

"You are right, you can't cook," Ellie said.

Louise groaned, "Ellie! You weren't supposed to say anything."

Jake laughed. It was a chuckle that was infectious. "She didn't have to," he said. "I suspect we'd have caught on quick with this kind of thing a few times a day." Going over to the stew, he took a sniff. "But this smells passable."

With another groan, Louise admitted, "It's all I can make."

"That's alright," Jake said. He reached onto a shelf and showed her a worn book. "This is a cookbook. It'll teach you everything you need to know. It's real easy," he said. "That's how I learned. I think there's even a biscuit recipe in there."

Louise picked it up and let it fall open to a page. She read and then hmmed. "Yes, that doesn't look too hard," she said.

There was a knock on the kitchen door and Jake went over to it. A boy handed him a thick envelope. Jake looked at it, thanked the boy with a tense voice, then turned.

The laughter had gone out of Louise. The look Jake wore sent chills down her spine.

Chapter 13

"You all start without me. I'll be back for supper shortly," Jake said, then he turned and left the room.

"Don't worry, he does that sometimes," Ellie said. "He's going to go to his locked room. But he'll be back."

"Locked room?" Louise asked, getting bowls from the cabinet.

"Yes. He goes there to work in quiet." Ellie jumped up and got the spoons, putting them on the table.

Just as Louise had set the filled bowls on the table, Jake reentered, looking as though nothing was wrong. She looked at him from the side of her eyes, but didn't ask. Whatever it was, it was obvious he didn't want the children to know.

"More story?" Phil asked.

"Why yes, I think we can tell another story at bedtime," Louise promised.

Ellie grinned. "I hope you become our ma so you can tell me stories every day. Molly Jefferson was wrong!"

Jake raised his eyebrows. Louise quickly explained Ellie's previous concern and he shook his head. "Not all little girls are so lucky when their pa gets a mail-order bride," he said. "So be nice to Molly. Maybe you can invite her over for a story."

Ellie nodded thoughtfully.

Jake spooned up a bite, tasted it and nodded. "Quite good. More than passable. Thank you, Louise."

She didn't answer, but met his eyes across the table. They were warm. He didn't seem upset, he seemed a man content, happy with his little family at dinner. For a moment, she wondered if this comfortable feeling was something she'd have every day. She liked it. It was…nice.

Once dinner finished, Louise set to washing the dishes. After another story and bedtime for the children, she wandered around to find Jake. Walking through the house, she didn't see or hear him, so she went down to the shop. It was dark, all but for a crack of light seeping out from under a door. She stood outside of it and hesitated, her hand raised to knock.

Shaking her head, Louise turned and walked back up to her room. Jake was right. Everyone had their secrets. She just wondered if she was wrong to have brought hers here. Ellie and Phil were sweet children, and she could see herself easily loving them. She already did, and it had only been a day. Would she grow to have those feelings for Jake, as well?

He seemed kind, which was more than she dared hope for. His handsome appearance didn't hurt, either. Louise was actually looking forward to spending more time with him.

Once in her room, she shut her door and brought her handbag to her bed. Opening it, she looked at the promissory notes one by one. There was nothing new to see. Still, she tried to puzzle out similarities. There had to be someone who could help her and Mathilda, but who?

Louise sighed. She couldn't continue to carry the notes with her everywhere she went. That wasn't safe. She put the papers back inside of the book, tied the ribbon around it, and slid it far back under her bed. There, that would do for now. No one was likely to come into her room, and if they did, they wouldn't be crawling under the bed.

Readying herself for sleep, Louise wondered how Mathilda was doing. Her sister was so sweet, she deserved a good man, and hopefully that's what this man in Midway was, good. Jake seemed like a good man, even though she realized he was hiding something. Still, it wasn't her business to know. She'd respect his secret and hoped he'd respect hers.

Jake hadn't asked about her past, which seemed a little strange, but either he didn't care or else he wasn't interested. Either way, she'd take it.

Though...she wished she could tell someone what had happened. Louise desperately hoped there was someone who could help. She wanted to stop

Mr. Hillcock. She also wanted to be rid of him forever.

Her troubled mind struggled to calm so she could fall asleep. Worries crowded her like too many passengers on a stagecoach. At last, just as the dawn was rising, she fell into a fitful sleep. Bleary eyed, she rose when she heard the children running down the hall.

Dressing, she quickly pinned her hair back and went downstairs. Jake was in the kitchen, and he looked as exhausted as she felt. They looked at each other and wordlessly recognized the look. Neither said anything. As she walked past him, Jake reached out and brushed his hand against hers.

Louise wasn't sure why, but it sent a tingle through her, and she turned and smiled at him. He captured her hand in his and was about to speak, when there was a knock at the door, and the same boy as the night before arrived, this time with a folded note.

Jake took it and shoved it in his pocket. "Louise," he said, "I know you've hardly gotten here, but would you be willing to take care of things at the store for a little while? I've some important work that can't wait."

"Of course," she answered.

He didn't say anything more, just turned and left.

Ellie watched from across the kitchen with a solemn look. "Pa's been getting real worried about something," she said. "It's good you're here now." The girl went back to her porridge Jake had made, drizzled heavily with honey, and Louise stared at the doorway Jake had gone through.

Something serious was happening. Could this be why he was so concerned about the children?

Was he also in trouble?

Chapter 14

Louise closed the shop ledger in satisfaction. Orderly rows of numbers were now all perfectly calculated. Gazing around the store with her hands on her hips, she surveyed her handiwork. The shelves were tidy, the candy jars full, and the customers gone for the day. It was hard work being there in the shop. She not only helped run it, but took care of the children too. Louise had never done so much in her life, but she was really enjoying it.

It was hard to believe that almost two weeks had passed. She was feeling quite at home there. Jake was enjoyable to be around. He was well read, something that surprised her. Not at all what she'd imagined a man who wanted a mail-order bride would be. It didn't matter what the subject was, he seemed familiar with it. From the law to novels, and the newspaper that he read every inch of, he seemed to absorb each detail and recall it later in conversation.

He intrigued her, and she wanted to know more about him, but it was hard. There wasn't much time. They were kept busy during the day at the shop, and in the evenings when it closed, he sometimes disappeared for hours. When he was there, they talked. Sometimes he explained things about running the store, other times he stared at her in such a way she could hardly form a sentence she felt so flustered.

That said, she didn't mind those moments at all, and actually looked forward to them.

At night, she was exhausted when she crawled into the small bed, but it was a good feeling. One of contentment. When it wasn't overrun with worry about Mathilda's welfare or Mr. Hillcock finding her.

Making her way to the kitchen, Louise put her hands on her hips and slowly read the cookbook's instructions. Whispering them aloud to herself, she mixed the flour, lard, salt, and water to form a dough.

Jake came in, whistling. "Ah, biscuits again?" he asked, trying to smooth the wince on his face.

"I'm going to get them right," Louise said firmly. "One day."

"I might run out of flour by that time," he winked, then laughed. "I put in an order for another ten barrels. Try to leave me at least two for customers, yeah?"

She couldn't help it, Louise laughed too, so much that she got tears in her eyes. "Oh you," she said. "Stop it. I'm going to try and get them right before we get to that point. I *might* even be able to leave you three barrels."

His laughter boomed, and he wiped tears from his eyes too. Louise got her mirth under control and turned back to the book. "Don't over mix," she muttered as she read.

Jake moved close and reached for an apple in a bowl nearby her. Every cell in her body could feel his nearness. She tried not to become distracted by his natural scent or the fact that he was just steps away, closer than he needed to be. Taking out his pocketknife, he sliced off a sliver of the apple. "Preacher comes back in a few days," he said, not looking at her.

Louise sucked in a breath. Neither of them had mentioned it, but the question had hung, unspoken, over them. Would he marry her? She finally looked up at Jake, to see he was looking at her. There was a strange expression on his face.

She couldn't tell if he was going to send her on her way or take her into his arms. Louise hoped it would be the second. The short time she'd been pressed against his chest when slipping off a short ladder in the store hadn't been long enough, and had haunted her memories since.

"Jake," she said, "I..." What could she say? That she wanted to stay? That she needed to stay? Louise was torn between selfishness and desire. But above all, she was worried each day about the danger she was putting this small family in. Would telling the truth help or hurt?

Jake put the apple down. "Listen," he cleared his throat. "I…"

Neither of them spoke. The air was heavy. Each searched the other's face. Louise felt this strong impulse to tell him. To tell him everything. Each moment from her escape to the fact she wanted to stay with him.

But she couldn't. How could a simple shopkeeper help her?

He went on, "Some things have happened the last few weeks that have made me…busier than usual. And I know I've been neglecting you and the children. It's not fair to you women, marrying men without even getting to know them first, and I'd hoped to show you how I was different. Unfortunately, between the store and this…extra work, I've not been able to do that."

"I understand," Louise said. She rested her hand on his arm. "Just you wanting to do that means a lot to me. You have no idea how nice it is to hear you say that."

Jake looked for a long moment at her hand. Nervously, she removed it. What was he about to tell her?

He sliced off another piece of apple. "I've been thinking."

He stopped again and Louise held her breath. He was quiet for so long, she finally asked, "Yes?"

"Well," Jake set down the apple and stared at it a moment before looking up at her.

His warm eyes were piercing, and his Adam's apple bobbed. Was he as nervous as she was? Louise had flutters in her stomach. She couldn't tell if they were a premonition of something bad, or of something good about to happen. All she knew was she couldn't bear the suspense much longer.

"I think I'd like to marry you," Jake blurted. He closed the distance between them. "The children love you, I'm attracted to you, and I've never known a woman to make cannonballs—I mean, biscuits quite the way you do. I suspect that means we might be a good match."

Louise couldn't help it. Her lips quirked. "You'd better watch it, mister, or those cannonballs might be aimed at your head."

Jake's warm laughter filled her ears, and he leaned in close, wrapping his arms around her. "That's what I love about you," he said, nuzzling his chin into the top of her head. "I can tell you're a woman to keep me on my toes, and I like that."

Louise tipped her head up slightly, and Jake brought his lower. "Jake," she said, taking the moment to breathe in deeply. His shaving soap was delicious, and she wondered if he tasted as good as he smelled. "I would be glad to marry you. I enjoy being around you and the children too."

Her lips were so close to his, if she just raised slightly on her toes they'd brush against his. Louise wondered how they'd feel. Would his kiss be warm and gentle? Hard and possessing?

The same thought must have been in Jake's mind, for he lowered his head slightly, and there was almost no distance between them. "Louise," he whispered.

His breath was warm, tickling her face. "Jake?" she asked.

"Almost Ma? You gonna kiss?"

Louise startled and Jake backed up quickly. They turned to see Ellie and Phil watching them, huge grins plastered on their faces.

"Ah, that is," Louise turned back to the biscuits, and began to drop them on the baking sheet. Unfortunately, they did sound a little like cannonballs as they fell.

Jake just winked at the children. "I'll open up the store," he said. "Bring me a few of those cannonballs when you're done, please."

"Oh you!" Louise said and looked around for something to throw at him. She aimed her dishtowel, but it fell far to the side, and with hardly any distance.

Ellie shook her head. "Looks like you need to learn to throw, too."

With a laugh that was half groan, Louise put the biscuits in the oven. They looked slightly better, didn't they? Dipping the ladle into the pot on the stove, she gave the children their oatmeal and drizzled plenty of maple syrup on top. Their grins up at her made her feel warm inside.

She couldn't wait for the children to meet Mathilda. She was sure her sister would love them as much as she did. Louise also couldn't wait for her to meet Jake. He wasn't rich, but he was handsome, and Louise could tell that there was an attraction growing between them. Something she'd never even dared hoped for in a marriage of any kind.

Humming to herself, she took off her apron, kissed the children, and went downstairs to help Jake.

The door to the shop was closing, and the same boy she'd seen several times now was leaving. Jake stood watching him, hastily shoving a note in his pocket.

"Everything alright?" Louise asked as she moved toward a carton of ribbon to unpack and set out.

"Just fine," Jake said with a frown. "You okay for a little by yourself?" he asked.

"Of course," she assured him.

As Jake turned and left, reaching into his pocket, Louise felt that familiar lump of worry wake up. Something was about to happen, something serious.

Chapter 15

Louise felt around under her bed. *A Lady's Book of Poetry* wasn't there. Feeling panicked, she felt around again. And again. What had happened to it? Where was it?

She pushed herself out from under the bed. Had she moved it and simply forgotten? It was unlikely, but quickly she opened the chest of drawers and thrust her hands in it. Swirling the clothes and other few belongings she had around, she felt her fear rising. Moving to the bed, she sat leaning forward, her head in her hands.

What could she do? If it was gone, she had no proof of the crime against her and Mathilda. She had nothing to protect either of them. It was only a matter of time before Mr. Hillcock found her, she knew it. Last night after talking with Jake, she realized that she wanted to stay, and she wanted to care for the children. So, she had formed a plan.

She'd give Mr. Hillcock an offer. She wouldn't turn over the promissory notes to the authorities on grounds of extortion and illegal activity, and he'd leave her and Mathilda alone. While Louise didn't know how to contact her sister, she was sure she'd figure that out. That she could feel deeply inside of her.

But now, there was no book. No promissory notes. No chance to keep them safe and away from Mr. Hillcock to keep him from bothering her or Mathilda.

The children. Louise's head snapped up. Perhaps one of the children had found it. She flung open her door and crashed right into Jake.

"I'm sorr—" Louise froze. In Jake's hand was the book. The ribbon had been retied. That wasn't the way she'd left it.

Her eyes flicked to it, and then back to Jake.

"We'd better talk," he said quietly. "I sent the kids to their room for a while."

Louise nodded. This was it. He was making her leave. What else did she expect? She'd been foolish. She'd done something dangerous and Jake was right. It was best for her to leave before harm came to the children. How had she been so inconsiderate as not to even think about that before she'd agreed to become the mail-order bride? Had she really hoped all would be well once she arrived?

A pang of regret struck her heart as she thought about Ellie and Phil. How would they handle the loss of a second mother figure, when they'd been so close to getting their new ma? Ellie especially.

"Follow me," he said, his voice low. Her stomach clenched, and Louise nodded, silently. Jake still held *A Lady's Book of Poetry*.

They went down the stairs, and to the closed door she'd seen the light under previously. Taking a key from his pocket, Jake unlocked the door and pointed inward. Swallowing the lump in her throat, Louise walked in, unsure what to expect.

Jake lit a small lantern, and Louise turned slowly, examining each wall. What she saw surprised her. One wall was filled with newspaper clippings. Another had photographs. She leaned closer and gasped. Her head jerked back to Jake and he nodded, then tapped her book.

"Before you say anything," he said, "I'm going to trust you enough to tell you a story. And then, I want the truth from you. If you're working with him, I want to know. You need to understand what's at stake. I told you the day we met how important it was to me to keep the children safe. I'm not going to have you put them at risk. What you say determines what we do next."

Louise drew her brows in confusion. "Working with him? With..." then she understood. When Jake saw the promissory notes, he must have thought she was Mr. Hillcock's accomplice. "Jake—"

"No. Me first," he said, and pointed to a chair. She sat, and he rested on a stool. He rocked it back slightly and said, "I've not been completely honest with you."

Louise didn't say anything. She wasn't sure she was supposed to. Jake continued, "About four years ago, I was hot on the trail of a criminal. He was some of everything. Con man. Blackmailer. Murderer. He preyed on the weak and the powerful. Somehow, he also always got away. I got close, real close to finding him, but then my identity was compromised. I managed to escape with only a bullet in my shoulder."

Louise's eyes darted toward the shoulder he pointed at.

"I found myself here, a small town. The perfect place to lie low for a while. Start over. Even better, there was a young widow. She knew my secret. Wrangled it out of me the night she asked me to marry her. That's right, she asked me," he said at her surprised expression. "Turned out she'd put out an ad, hoping for a man to help run the store and care for her and her daughter, plus her baby on the way.

"I didn't like the idea. I didn't want to put her at risk, or her children, but it was the perfect cover. So, I became Jake, her new husband. We concocted a story about having been childhood sweethearts. Everyone bought it. What I didn't expect, however, was for her to die just a few weeks after we married. Ellen, Ellie's named after her, got real sick after she had Phil. The doc tried, but he couldn't help her. Then it was me, a four-year-old, and a newborn baby."

Louise longed to interrupt, but she didn't. Instead, she listened, her heart aching as each of the pieces fell together. This explained why the children looked nothing like him, but they were so young, they likely knew no other father.

"To keep the children safe, I stayed undercover. 'Contact me only when you need me,' I told them. And about a month before you came, they did."

"Who?" Louise finally burst out. "Who contacted you? Who do you work for?"

"The FBI," Jake said. "I'm an agent."

Louise drew a breath. This humble shopkeeper was an FBI agent? She knew she was staring at him now. It felt like her eyes were about to burst out of their sockets.

"That's when I knew I had to do something. That man," he pointed to a photograph of Mr. Hillcock, "has set foot in the States, not something he has done but once in the last few years. And I'm not sure why, but I do know he's coming this way. Intel reached me saying he's pretty close by and they need me to learn what I can and slow him until he's intercepted. Now, that's why I have to ask you. Are you working with him? Did you lead him here?"

"No," Louise said, in a shaky breath, staring right at him. "And yes."

Jake tensed, and she held up a hand. "I promise you I'm not working with him. However, I might be the reason he is on his way here. You saw my book. You know what's in it."

He nodded. "Ellie had it. She wanted to read and become a lady, she said. I didn't know it was yours until I opened it and saw the papers inside. Care to explain those?"

"I guess I'm going to have to," Louise said. "It's the only way to prove my innocence, and my guilt."

"That's right," Jake said. "And we don't have long." He jerked his thumb to the photo of Mr. Hillcock on the wall. "He's on the train set to arrive here this evening."

Chapter 16

Louise closed her eyes, but only for a moment. It was already late afternoon. There might not even be time to get through her story. She had no idea when the train was coming in. Steeling herself, she looked right into Jake's eyes.

"When I got here and you didn't ask about my past, I was surprised. And grateful. The reason I didn't give you my last name is I am trying to hide, too."

Jake was sitting, arms crossed, his face blank. She continued. "My mother died when I was in finishing school. You may have overheard me telling Ellie that. I had to come home because around the same time, my father's lawyer said we were having financial difficulties. My younger sister, Mathilda, had a governess who was dismissed, so I became her teacher."

"Mathilda?" Jake reached into his pocket and pulled out a note. "Mathilda Weston?"

"Yes," Louise gasped, jumping up and nearly falling over in her haste to see the scrap. "Is she hurt? Is she well?"

Jake tapped a finger on the table. "This was actually a message from her own mail-order husband. He's the chief of police in Midway."

Louise sat down again in surprise. "A police chief? Thank goodness," she sighed. "She'll be safe. I hope."

Jake said, "I'll explain more about what he wants, but I want to hear your story first."

She nodded. "Well, a few years later, Father died. By then, we were very badly off. The house needed repairs, and there was little money for food, let alone anything else. Mattie—Mathilda—and I took in work. Sewing, laundry. I tried to become a governess, but not having references, and not having completed finishing school, no one would hire me. It didn't help that our once well-off family was in disgrace, after Father supposedly drank and gambled away all the money."

Louise stood and paced for a moment as best as she could in the tiny room. She hated this part of the story. Turning to face Jake, she bit her lip, willing herself to hold back the tears that wanted to be shed.

"Father's lawyer proposed a solution. He suggested marriage and said he knew someone, a businessman. This businessman was well off, and things would improve for me financially, and also allow me a better status, so I could ensure a good match for Mathilda. A love match, not a desperation match, like I was being forced to choose. From the start, I hated the idea. Mattie never knew that. I pretended to be delighted, but I wasn't. Still, it was the only way I might be able to provide for her."

Jake was nodding slowly, his fingers still drumming on the note with Mathilda's name. Louise could hardly take her eyes off of it. "Go on," he said. "This man you were to marry, is him?" He pointed again to the wall.

Mr. Hillcock's cold gaze stared at her and she shuddered. "Yes. It was arranged by Father's lawyer for Mattie and me to meet him in England. We were to be wed there, and board the *Titanic* for our honeymoon. Mattie would travel back home, and I would hopefully meet some young man on our honeymoon to introduce her to."

Blinking several times, Jake leaned forward. "The *Titanic*? The *Titanic*?" He seemed shocked, and Louise nodded.

"Yes. And I promise to give you every detail of that later, but it appears time is not something we have a lot of, and I've much more to tell you."

Nodding, he leaned back again. Swallowing hard, Louise wrapped her arms tightly around herself as she sat again on the chair. "We arrived in England and were taken to a hotel suite. We were also instructed to stay in it. That afternoon, Mr. Hillcock came to the room. He was so cold. So hard. He was belittling in his speech. If I flattered, he gave me smiles. If I asked a question, he scolded me. He said," she closed her eyes and drew a shaky breath, "he expected perfection from me, and he would rid me of what he didn't like, even if he must beat it out of me."

"That monster," Jake said, letting out a quiet swear. He looked up at her, "Forgive me. The idea that anyone would hurt you, or even think about hurting you, makes me angry."

Her voice trembling, Louise continued, "That night, we had dinner with him and his business associate, a Mr. Longsmith. All throughout dinner, I kept thinking I'd seen his companion. When we returned to the room, I remembered where. There had been a drawing of him in the newspaper. He and his accomplice were wanted in connection to multiple crimes.

"Just as I whispered it to Mattie, Mr. Hillcock came into our room. He said he had business to take care of, and I was to meet him on the ship in the morning. We'd get married on board. In that moment, I knew this was our chance for escape, and I didn't know if there'd be another. He set his briefcase down to write a note."

Louise dropped her head into her hands. "I don't know why I did it, but I don't regret it. His briefcase had become unlatched, and I could see a thick pile of cash, both American and British, in there. So, I reached in and took a large portion of it. I got those as well," she gestured to the poetry book, "and once he left, we made plans to escape, for he had given me the *Titanic* tickets."

"I wonder why, a man like that," Jake said, rubbing at his jaw.

"I wondered that too," Louise said. "I was not about to argue it, though. The names on the tickets were not ours, and later, I wondered if the tickets were stolen, or won in a gamble. It was perfect, though, a chance to hide and paid for transportation back to the United States."

"What happened then?" he asked, leaning forward slightly.

"We packed, and the next morning I sent our bags to the *Titanic*. Mattie and I left, and I had her send the telegrams—one to you that I was coming and one to her man, and then I went shopping."

"Shopping?" Jake's tone was one of absolute surprise.

"Shopping," she agreed. "I bought a man's shirt, trousers, jacket, and hat, and changed into them." At his stunned look, she added, "Trousers are quite comfortable, really. You men are lucky."

Jake's mouth moved, but nothing came out. Grinning at his expression, she continued, "We boarded, Mattie and I, and it was then that I discovered the pieces of paper I'd grabbed were promissory notes. As we were sorting through them, I discovered one that was very upsetting. May I?" she asked, gesturing to the book.

Jake pushed it over to her. She opened the false book and flipped through until she found the note with her and Mathilda's names. She handed it to him and he read it silently, then looked up at her.

"Yes. Father, or his lawyer, I don't know which, sold me and Mathilda to Mr. Hillcock and his associate."

When Jake didn't say anything, she continued. "We were on the *Titanic* when she struck the iceberg. Mattie and I got onto a lifeboat and were later rescued by the *Carpathia*, which took us to New York. Once there, immediately we took the train west, for you see, while I'd hoped that we'd be presumed lost at sea, in her exhaustion, my sister gave our real names and they were printed in the newspaper."

"And that's why you didn't want to give it to me?" Jake asked.

"Yes. Now, you've heard my story. Judge me how you will. I deserve whatever punishment you see fit for endangering the children." Louise raised her chin in acceptance, yet begged, "But will you please tell me what's in that note from my sister?"

Chapter 17

After a long moment of staring at her, Jake nodded. "There are two notes. The first says: "Looking for mail-order bride whose sister went to Midway. She has papers we must have. Send to Chief of Police of Midway, Ky."

"And there's a second?" Louise asked.

Jake pulled it out. "It came the next day." He read, "Caught Longsmith, AKA Long John. Shot Midway Chief of Police. Older sister in danger. Watch for Hillcock."

"Shot? Is he alive? Is my sister hurt?" Louise jumped up again.

"I don't know," Jake said, dropping the notes and resting his elbows on the table. He ran his fingers through his hair, over his face, and sighed. "I sent a message for more information. I'm sure I'll hear back soon. But it seems that he's found you and he's on his way. Now, he's the man I've been after for a long time, so I don't know if I should be mad you brought him here and blew my cover and put the children at risk, or if I should be grateful and kiss you."

Louise's head snapped up. A long moment passed between them before she spoke, staring at him boldly. "I'd rather you kiss me."

Taken aback, Jake growled, "I'm going to do that, mark my words."

She shivered, but this time it wasn't in fear. Without looking away, Louise smiled at him. The very air seemed charged with an electric current. He moved forward slightly, and she wondered if he'd kiss her now.

But he seemed to catch himself, for he picked up *A Lady's Book of Poetry* and frowned at it. She asked, "What do we do now? It seems we both had secrets, and we both wanted to put away the same man. It also appears that you have the means to do it. So, how can we make that happen, without disclosing who you are? And what aid can we give to my sister?"

Jake reached out and took her hand, pulling her upward. He laced his fingers through hers, a surprisingly intimate movement that Louise didn't mind at all.

"That's what I'm working on," he said. "I'm not completely sure, but I think I might have a plan." He met her eyes, but didn't release her hand. "I need you to make me a promise, though."

"Anything," Louise promised, moving closer to him.

The static in the air was undeniable. She was so close, she could smell the scented soap he'd used to wash with, and something else—warm, comforting, and delicious. It made her want to close the distance and claim him for herself, just as she longed for him to claim her.

Jake swallowed hard. "Woman," he growled, "you make it hard for a man to concentrate."

A hint of a smile formed, and Louise tilted her head down, but looked up at him through her lashes. "Is that so?" she asked.

Drawing her close, Jake buried his nose in her neck and breathed in deeply. "Louise," he said quietly. "The man you were to marry is dangerous. He's killed before and he might do it again. If something were to happen to me, and to you, the children would be alone."

As he stepped back, pain in his eyes, Louise nodded. She understood.

"I will keep the children safe," she promised. "But…" Louise allowed the tear to fall, even as she lifted her chin, "you must return to me as well, Jake. Fate brought both of us here, to this place, and I won't let destiny divide us."

Jake kissed her then, and the kiss was everything Louise had dreamed of and more. It ended far too quickly, and she looked up, breathlessly, to see Jake's chest rising and falling rapidly, and his breath uneven.

He stepped away and opened the door and she followed him into the shop. Jake locked the door behind him, then handed her the key. "I've a spare," he said. "But if something happens, make sure all of this gets to the FBI. Once Hillcock is taken care of, I'll send all that's needed to Midway to help your sister."

Louise nodded.

The train's whistle blew, signaling to the town the arrival of its passengers. Louise and Jake looked at each other. He strode over and locked the door shop, then put on a thick leather vest.

"Not enough to stop a bullet," he said, "but it will help. If I don't make it, call it a robbery, and get the FBI. Do you understand? I've men on the way. They'll take care of Hillcock if I don't, if they can get here in time."

"Wait," Louise said. "I want a pistol too. If they aren't here in time, I need to protect the children."

His eyes not leaving hers, Jake reached under the counter and handed her the gun. "Do you know how to use it?" he asked.

Taking it, she gave a small nod. "I'm full of surprises," she said. Louise moved toward the stairs and looked over her shoulder. "He won't be taking me or harming the children. If he gets past you, I'll stop him myself."

Chapter 18

"Children, we are going to draw pictures," Louise said. She went into the children's room, with Ellie and Phil close behind her. She took their box of crayons and then some sheets of paper into the corner of the room, the one farthest from the door.

"I wish I had these when I was a girl," she said cheerfully as she took out a crayon. "Eight beautiful colors to draw with! Why, you can draw almost anything," she said.

Phil sat down and started scribbling. "Let's see if we can each cover an entire page with artwork," Louise said, placing herself between the door and the children. "Later, I'll tack them up on the wall so I can admire your lovely drawings."

"What about dinner?" Ellie asked.

Louise hadn't thought of that. It was getting close to time to eat. Usually, she'd be in the kitchen right now, attempting to make something edible. "I'll bring you something," she said brightly. "We'll have a picnic in here, isn't that silly?"

The kids laughed at the idea, and Louise quickly went to the kitchen. She grabbed apples, cheese, and some cookies Jake had helped her make and took them back upstairs. The children eagerly ate, while Louise split her attention between them, and any noises below where the shop was.

Only a single door separated the upstairs from the down, and she couldn't hear anything, but a feeling of wrongness fell over her. If Mr. Hillcock had known to go to this town, he might have someone locally working for him or passing along information. That same person might just know the layout of the building they were in, as well as how Jake might defend himself. The idea concerned her.

"Ellie," Louise said quietly. "I'll be right back. I want you to stay in this room and not leave. No

matter what, do you hear me?" At the little girl's
nod, she continued, "And if you hear any loud
noises, the two of you get up under your bed and
pretend to be asleep."

"Are you going to be alright?" Ellie asked, her
eyes wide.

"Yes," Louise said firmly. "But I'm not sure how
long it will be before I come back. Promise me
you'll be quiet and stay here."

At the girl's solemn nod, Louise kissed each of
the children on the tops of their heads, held her
first finger to her lips, and crept over to the door
and into the hallway. She put her hand on the knob
and slowly turned it, opening it just a crack and
hoping it wouldn't make any noise. From below,
she could hear men talking. There was more than
one stranger, and Jake.

"Sorry, yes, she was here. Sent her on her way,
though. She wasn't good enough to be a mother.
Did you know she can't even cook? That's not
what I asked for in my advertisement."

"We were told she's still here," Mr. Hillcock's
voice said, smooth and oily. "Her sister is terribly

sick. I've come to take her to see her, and perhaps say goodbye."

Louise could imagine Jake rubbing at his chin and shaking his head as he answered, "No idea. Didn't even know about a sister. That's the problem with these mail-order brides. You never know what you're going to get."

"Enough."

Louise furrowed her brow in concentration, but she didn't recognize the new voice. "My men have been watching for you, boss. She's not left. She's probably upstairs with the brats."

"Kids, huh?" Mr. Hillcock's voice became amused. "Well, that changes things. Tell us where she is, and I won't hurt the kids. I'll even drop them off at the church after I kill you."

Anger flared in Louise, but she knew that she was trapped upstairs. There was no way to leave and get help. She also couldn't get the children out. She closed the door as quietly as she could and locked it. Her head swiveling, she grabbed the chair from her room and wedged it under the doorknob.

Dashing back into the children's room, she whispered, "Under the bed, now. Don't come out, whatever you do."

Ellie looked at her fearfully, and Louise realized she'd drawn the pistol and the children could see it. "No harm will come to you," she promised. "Your pa is trying to hold off some bad men robbing the store. If they come up here, I won't let them hurt you."

Ellie nodded. She took the food under the bed with her and Phil, and fed him small bites to keep him quiet. Louise leaned down and whispered, "I'm going to shut your door. I'll be hiding in the hallway. I won't let them in, but stay quiet."

She closed the door behind her and pressed herself into the back corner of the hallway behind a small chair. From her vantage point, she could see whoever came up the stairs, but they wouldn't see her until it was too late.

Crouched down, Louise looked at the pistol and willed her hands to stop trembling. From downstairs there was a shout, a crashing sound, and then a gunshot.

Phil made a noise, but Ellie must have shushed him, for he was quiet again. Louise raised the pistol, ready to take aim. She waited, but it was quiet. Too quiet.

Several long, slow minutes passed. No one came up the stairs. Louise crept forward, toward the door to the stairs and the shop. Maybe Jake had taken care of Mr. Hillcock. Maybe his men had come. Slowly twisting the knob, she slipped down the stairs one step at a time, the pistol tight in her grip.

As she drew closer, she heard nothing, and summoning her courage, peered around the corner to the shop.

There, before her, was Jake, tied up, and Mr. Hillcock pointing his pistol at her.

Chapter 19

"I knew you'd never be able to resist the silence," he said with his cold smile. "Women are so easy to fool. I also know there are two children upstairs and you don't want anything to happen to them. Be a good girl, and set down your weapon."

Louise slowly set it down on the wooden shop floorboards and waited. Her eyes flicked to Jake. There was blood on his face, but other than that, he looked well. She wondered why no townsfolk were nearby. Didn't they hear the noise?

"I have come for the papers," Mr. Hillcock said. "My associate here, is a reverend. He's going to wed us after you hand them to me."

"I won't be marrying you," Louise said, raising her chin in defiance.

"Not even to spare the lives of the innocents you dragged into this?" he asked.

Louise's mind whirled. It was true. She had dragged them into it. But there had to be a way out. She remembered what Jake had said, his men were on the way. Perhaps she could buy them time to arrive. "Why would you still want to marry me?" she asked.

"Because, my dear," Mr. Hillcock answered, "I took out a life insurance policy on you. It's only good once we are married."

"And then what?" Louise asked. "You'll get rid of me?" She didn't have to pretend, her voice trembled with fear.

He shrugged. "Perhaps. Or perhaps your good behavior is what will keep your little sister safe."

Louise looked down at the ground, pretending submission. That was what he liked. She had to stall him. But how long would it take for help to arrive?

"I will get them," she said. "They are...on my person." She glanced up at Mr. Hillcock, then at his associate. "I…I would like privacy please. I can just use the back storage room to remove them and hand them over."

"And allow you to get another weapon? I don't think so, Miss Weston," Mr. Hillcock said.

"There's no other way out, boss. Should be fine," the other man said. He added with a sneer, "Spoiled rich girls are all the same, even when they aren't rich anymore. They're all talk, but in the end, they give us what we want."

After a moment, Mr. Hillcock nodded, a smirk forming. "You're right. I've seen that many times. Fine. You have one minute. Take any longer, and I go upstairs and look for the children."

Louise nodded and hurried to the back room. Outside the room, she could hear Mr. Hillcock counting.

"One…two…three…"

Her eyes raced as she looked for something to defend herself with or else distract them longer. A catalogue rested on a shelf, and an idea sprang to her mind. Perhaps she could play along a little more with that idea of being a useless woman.

"…forty-one… forty-two…"

Louise tore several pages loose, then ripped them until they were the size of the promissory notes.

"…fifty-six…"

She opened the door then, holding the bundle of paper in her hand. "I have them."

Mr. Hillcock stepped toward her, a greedy look on his face as he stared at her hand.

"Can I assume," Louise asked, trying to summon his attention, "that these are important?"

"Just give them to me," he snarled, reaching for them.

"No." Louise stepped back. From her other hand, she pulled out a booklet of matches and struck one. She held it close. Mr. Hillcock hissed, "What are you doing, you fool?"

"Negotiating," Louise said, holding the match closer. "I've had no say in this marriage since the beginning. It's time for you to hear what I'd like out of it. Kill me now, we aren't married. Threaten me, I burn the papers."

Mr. Hillcock's eyes darted between her face and the papers. Behind him, Jake had been wiggling.

He'd managed to get one of his hands almost loose. She had to distract Mr. Hillcock just a little longer. Her eyes flicked to the window and the street beyond, then back to Mr. Hillcock.

The short glance had shown three men in suits with rifles, moving in slowly. Those must be Jake's men. They were here!

Mr. Hillcock moved closer, anger on his face. Louise did the only thing she knew to distract him. She acted every bit as spoiled and entitled as she could muster.

"I want dresses," she screeched, and stomped her foot.

The sudden tone and switch of her voice startled all three men. Jake looked at her in alarm, while Mr. Hillcock froze. "Wh-what did you say?"

"Dresses. I want dresses. You think I will marry you and be poor? I want dresses. A new one each month. And matching shoes." Louise pushed her lip out and tried to do her best pout. She was very out of practice. It had been years since she'd done one. It probably looked as dreadful as her biscuits.

"Yes, yes, of course," he said, eyes never leaving the bundle in her hand. "Just give me those."

Louise took another step back. Could she lead him further away from Jake?

"I want a cook," she said, "and a housekeeper. Mr. Brown promised all of those things. He said you'd give me everything I wanted! You've said nothing about anything you'll give me. Of course, I ran. I expect the lifestyle I was told I'd get."

By this point, Mr. Hillcock stared at her, his face one of puzzlement. "I...yes, of course. Dresses. Servants. Just...let me have those. You'll have whatever you like."

"You didn't have to threaten me," Louise said, allowing large tears to fall from her eyes. Letting out a hiccupping sob, she lowered her hands and slumped her shoulders forward as though she was giving in. Behind Mr. Hillcock, Jake was sawing at the rope around his feet and remaining tied hand with a pocketknife.

Hurry, Jake! She wasn't sure how much longer she could do this act. If Mr. Hillcock got much closer, he'd see the papers weren't real.

Mr. Hillcock glanced at his associate who shrugged. He reached out his hand, and Louise raised hers to hand him the papers just as the front window shattered, and the three men in suits burst through.

Louise fell to the ground, shielding her head with her arms. All around her there was scuffling and shouting, but no more gunshots. Someone touched her shoulder, crouching beside her, and she peered through her fingers.

"Jake!" she gasped, reaching out to grab him.

"It's over," he said, wrapping his arms around her and helping her stand. "They've caught him. You got him distracted and off center so they could get him."

Louise watched as the three men, and several others she recognized from the town, dragged Mr. Hillcock and his associate out of the store and down the street.

"We'll call it a robbery," Jake said quietly. "That's all the townsfolk need to know. The FBI promised to pay for the glass window, and anything damaged."

Louise nodded and looked around at the store. It was partially destroyed. Foodstuffs lay all over the floor, and the spools of ribbon she'd displayed so carefully were unwound and laying in the shattered glass. A large jar of peppermints had tipped over and spilled out, and were crunched into the wooden floor from shoes stepping on them.

"This will be a mess to clean," Louise said, then stopped as she realized her voice was shaky. So were her hands.

"We'll get it in time," Jake said. He looked her over. "You alright?"

"Yes," Louise whispered. She brought a hand to his face and ran it over his cheeks. "What of you? I see blood."

Jake shrugged. "I've had worse. They didn't do too much to me. I'm sorry I didn't get them. They surprised me. I was watching for Mr. Hillcock, when his associate was the one who came in and distracted me. Should have known better." He shook his head wryly. "I'm a little out of practice."

Louise dropped her hand to his chest and left it there. "I need to check on the children," she said.

He nodded, but grabbed her hand, holding it close to him. "Louise," he said.

"Jake?"

"I can't give you a cook, though we all know we need one," he teased, "and a housekeeper isn't in the stars, but a dress a month and matching shoes I could probably do, if you'll just marry me, Louise Weston."

The proposal was so unexpected she gasped and wrapped her arms around Jake in happiness. "Yes, Jake, yes," she laughed. "I don't need any of those things. I have all I want. I have you, and Ellie, and Phil."

Jake lowered his head and kissed her, then pulled back. "Let's do it tomorrow," he said. "We've waited long enough."

Louise stood on her tiptoes and pulled herself closer to him. "Tomorrow," she agreed, kissing him again.

Her heart was near bursting with joy. There were no more secrets to hide from, just a new life filled with love to look forward to.

Epilogue

Two years later

Louise peered in the oven door. It wasn't looking so good.

"How'd they turn out, Ma?" Ellie asked, walking into the kitchen.

"Not good," Louise said grimly. She pulled the biscuits out of the oven. "I don't understand," she complained. "I follow the recipe exactly, every time."

Ellie scrunched her nose and shook her head. "You'd think after over two years of making these, you'd get better. I'll tell Pa to order more flour next delivery."

"No need." Jake's voice startled them. With a grin, he walked in with baby Tilly. "We've got someone here who is going to give your ma cooking lessons."

"Is that so?" Louise said coolly, straightening up. She raised her chin and gave Jake her best scowl.

"It's so," Mathilda said, coming in from behind Jake and setting down a traveling bag. "My nieces and nephew can't live off stew and flapjacks alone."

"Mattie!" Louise cried and ran over to her sister. "When did you come? I thought it wouldn't be until tomorrow."

"I got an early train," Mathilda said, taking baby Tilly from Jake. "I couldn't wait another moment to see the baby you named after me." She cooed over the baby, then handed her back.

"Right. Lou, Ellie." Mathilda's voice was brisk. "Roll up your sleeves and hand me an apron."

With a grin, Ellie ran off to grab an apron for her aunt.

"I'm not that bad of a cook," Louise muttered. She shook the cookbook at Mathilda. "Look! I can make four things out of here."

"Oh?"

"Yes!" Louise started turning the pages.

Ellie returned, and ticked off her fingers, "Flapjacks, stew, porridge, and oatmeal. Good thing Pa owns a store. We eat a lot from there."

Louise laughed sheepishly, but it was true. They did.

"We've got a lot of work to do," Mathilda said solemnly. "Ellie, my sister is quite hopeless in the kitchen, though she's brilliant in many other ways. It's all up to you. Pay close attention."

Standing close to her aunt, Ellie copied her movements, while Louise stood back and watched. Jake set Tilly down in her basket in the kitchen and Phil dangled a stuffed rabbit with long ears overtop of her. Coming to stand behind her, Jake wrapped his arms around Louise.

As she leaned back into him, Louise looked up at Jake and smiled. "Thank you," she said.

Jake raised an eyebrow. "For what?"

Louise smiled. "For everything. For rescuing me, for marrying me, for giving me the perfect family, and helping my sister. I only wish I'd told you my secret sooner."

With a sigh and an exaggerated, mournful shake of his head, Jake said, "I wonder if I should have told you mine. I've got one more I've been keeping."

Alarmed, Louise twisted and looked at him. "What is it?"

Jake leaned close and whispered, "I have never liked biscuits."

Jerking back, Louise opened and closed her mouth. "You mean…this whole time…"

She spun and faced her sister. "Mattie. Bread, teach me to make bread. I never want to see another biscuit in my life," she declared, as Jake's laughter filled the room.

Did you enjoy Louise's story? Mathilda's adventure is also available in eBook, paperback, and large print. Find it today on Amazon.

Matilda gets on the Titanic, with only a small bag and a telegram receipt from the hastily penned note letting one Logan Fitzwick know she'd be delighted to be his wife.

Just a few days prior, she'd been giggling with her sister as they looked through the newspaper, wondering what kind of woman would be a mail-order bride. Now she knew—desperate.

Thank you for taking the time to read Louise!

Could I ask for one small favor? Reviews like yours on Amazon mean so much to me and help others to find my books! Even if it's just a few words, it means a lot!

There's also more to this series! Check out the Amazon Series Page for Rescue Me for more incredible stories!

Stop by my website to see everything I've written and keep up to date!
www.sarahlambbooks.com

Want more of Sarah's books? She writes for children and adults! Find them all on Amazon! Here are just a few!

Fiction for Adults

Caroline (Runaway Brides of the West Series)

The Christmas Treasure (Holiday Cottage Series)

Mathilda (Rescue Me: Mail-order Brides Series)

Louise (Rescue Me: Mail-order Brides Series)

A Second Chance in Pumpkin City (Pumpkin City series)

An Angel for Alice: A Christmas Eve Short Story

A Second Chance for Beatrice: A Christmas Eve Short Story

A Gunslinger for Grace (Mail-order Papa series)

Frances (Women of the Blue Ridge Series)

About Author

Sarah Lamb is the mother of two boys and wife to a teacher. She spends her days writing and editing books in the beautiful Shenandoah Valley.